"How are yo

"I'm fine."

"Glad to hear it."

The look Ty gave her, so warm and caring, made Claire stir the batter with a little more force than necessary. Made her think maybe he was more attractive than she'd originally thought.

His look made her feel as if she was missing something. Made her remember that once upon a time she believed in dreams and fairy tales. In happily-ever-afters.

No way was she ever going down that path again.

Dear Reader,

I've got a story for you. A few years ago, one of my critique partners suggested that our writing group think about helping some women in a homeless shelter. Instead of just writing a check, she thought we should give them gift bags full of all kinds of things we take for granted. Things like toothpaste, shampoo, lotion, soap and combs.

The five of us gathered up these items, and one evening we put together fifty bags for Christmas. We had so much fun, we've done it several times since.

Well, then we heard the most amazing thing. Last Mother's Day, those ladies had some bags left over. They took the extra bags and handed them out to women who were living on the streets...women less fortunate than themselves. Those are some pretty incredible ladies.

Kind of like the heroine of this book, Claire Grant.

Some of you might remember meeting Claire in my novel *Simple Gifts*. In *Simple Gifts* she was a homeless mom trying to get back on her feet. Claire and her story resonated with a lot of readers. With me, too! I couldn't forget Claire, and I knew she and her son, Wes, needed their own happy ending.

I spend most of my days writing, volunteering and being a wife and mother. I'm so thankful that Harlequin has given me the opportunity to write and dream about people I would like to be. Thanks so much for picking up my book. I hope you'll enjoy Claire's story. And if you have time, I hope you'll tell me what you think. Please visit me either at eHarlequin.com, or at www.shelleygalloway.com.

Shelley

The Mommy Bride

SHELLEY GALLOWAY

TORONTO • NEW YORK • LONDON
AMSTERDAM • PARIS • SYDNEY • HAMBURG
STOCKHOLM • ATHENS • TOKYO • MILAN • MADRID
PRAGUE • WARSAW • BUDAPEST • AUCKLAND

ISBN-13: 978-0-373-75216-4
ISBN-10:   0-373-75216-4

THE MOMMY BRIDE

ABOUT THE AUTHOR

Shelley Galloway loves to get up early, drink too much coffee and write books. These pastimes come in handy during her day-to-day life in southern Ohio. Most days she can be found driving her kids to their activities, writing romances in her basement or trying to find a way to get ahead of her pile of laundry. She's also been known to talk to her miniature dachshund Suzy as if she actually has opinions about books.

Shelley is the proud recipient of a *Romantic Times BOOKreviews* Reviewer's Choice Award for her 2006 release, *Simple Gifts*. Shelley attends several conferences every year and loves to meet readers. She also spends a lot of time online. Please visit her at eHarlequin.com or at www.shelleygalloway.com.

Books by Shelley Galloway

HARLEQUIN AMERICAN ROMANCE

Don't miss any of our special offers. Write to us at the following address for information on our newest releases.

Harlequin Reader Service
U.S.: 3010 Walden Ave., P.O. Box 1325, Buffalo, NY 14269
Canadian: P.O. Box 609, Fort Erie, Ont. L2A 5X3

To women who've struggled over adversity. And to women who've helped others achieve their dreams.

And, of course, to Tom.
For not blinking an eye when I buy fifty bars of soap for strangers…or when he discovers that yet again I forgot to do the laundry.

Chapter One

"I knew things were too good to be true," Lynette pronounced just as a young woman, a little girl and a teen tromped into the reception area of the Lane's End Memorial Hospital. "I was a fool to think we'd actually have a slow afternoon for once."

"We had a good forty-five minutes of downtime, that's got to be a record," Claire said as she hopped off her stool. "We almost got our crossword done."

"Almost." Lynette quickly shoved their daily crossword to one side as the trio approached, each wearing looks of worry and panic.

Closer inspection revealed a bloody towel wrapped around the boy's hand. Joking was pushed aside as duty clicked in. "May I help you?"

Treating them to a weary smile, the woman nodded. "Taylor here cut up his hand pretty bad. I think he's going to need some stitches."

The little girl's hair was the exact shade of auburn as the woman's; she stared at Claire. "We need some help."

Privately, Claire thought they all did. Their coats

weren't thick enough to ward off the cold weather. Each looked in need of hot soup. And as a slight musty scent floated her way, Claire realized that a shower would be a good idea, too.

A shiver ran through her as she fought back memories. Remembering darker times would do her no good now. She'd do well to keep that in mind. "We'll get you started in a jiffy," Claire promised with a smile, though she felt herself getting a little woozy. There was a lot of blood on that towel. "Lynette, I'll start the paperwork."

Her partner picked up a phone. "I'll go ahead and call for assistance."

After grabbing a clipboard holding the necessary forms, Claire guided the trio to a nearby cubicle. "We're calling for help so Taylor can get treated right away. In the meantime, we just need some basic information."

Wariness fought with relief in the woman's hazel eyes. "I don't have insurance."

Claire hadn't thought she did. In her experience, insurance premiums weren't high on your list when you didn't know where the next meal was coming from. "We'll worry about that in a bit. Just fill out what you can and we'll concentrate on getting Taylor fixed up."

The little girl's eyes widened just before she popped her thumb in her mouth. Tenderness passed over the woman's expression as she turned to Taylor, who was sitting in the chair next to her. Gently she combed back a lock of hair. "We did the right thing, didn't we?"

He still hadn't said a word. The woman didn't look like she needed an answer.

That was worrisome. As the woman started filling out

the forms, Claire glanced back toward her reception partner. "Lynette? Any word?"

"Yep." Behind her, Lynette was talking on the phone in her usual no-nonsense way, chomping gum in between every other word. "I got put on hold for a sec, but—here we go." Her voice a little louder, she said, "We're gonna need some help over here in registration. Yes. Uh-huh. Thank you."

"Any minute now," Claire promised. Funny how it seemed like things were taking forever, when in truth the trio had only arrived minutes ago.

As the girl sucked her thumb and the boy said nothing, Claire did what she could to try and provide reassurance. "Everything's going to be okay," she said. "The doctors are good here. And the staff's the best."

Some of the stress in the woman's eyes settled. A dash of kindness really did work wonders. Once their gazes met, Claire spoke slowly again. Remembering her son's last scrape, worn like a badge of honor, she said, "So, how'd you get cut?"

But that question didn't achieve the results she'd hoped for. Instead of an explanation, all she got was a suspicious look. Finally—almost defiantly—he mumbled, "I cut it on a can."

The woman's chin rose a bit. "We were…collecting cans and one had a torn edge."

Claire's wooziness increased tenfold. And not because of the blood. Unfortunately, she knew all about collecting cans in the dark. Swallowing hard, she fought to keep her voice neutral. "We'll get you fixed up in no time." She darted another look to the reception desk.

Lynette raised two fingers. "Two minutes, tops."

Claire touched the woman's arm again. "Let's go have a seat. I'll need to take you over to the—" Her words faded as the staff door to her left opened and she saw who arrived.

Ty Slattery.

Of course *he* had to be the one to come to provide assistance.

If she could, she'd cue movie trailer music and one of those announcers with a big, booming voice. *Just when she thought things couldn't get any worse...*

"Hey, Claire," Ty said as he approached.

"Hi, um, Dr. Slattery. We've, um, got a little issue here." She groaned inwardly at her awkwardness.

"My son got cut pretty bad," the woman said.

Ty didn't even blink at the soaked towel. "You sure did. I think you came to the right place," he said, his voice caring and kind. "I'm Dr. Slattery. Who are all of you?"

The mom blinked. "I'm Deanna Johns. This is Taylor. And this little thing is Annie."

"Nice to meet you," Ty replied, just like they were at the park instead of the hospital.

Claire sighed. Honestly, did he have to be so perfect? Time and again she'd seen Ty Slattery work magic with everyone who came in contact with him. For a man who wasn't all that heart-stoppingly handsome, he sure had a way with women.

When Dr. Slattery faced her, he pointed to the hallway on the opposite side of the room. "I was just about to leave for the day when I heard Lynette's page. Thought I'd see if I could help out."

She knew she should tell him thanks.

She knew she should smile back at him. But that felt almost impossible to do. He affected her too much.

Luckily he was ignoring her rudeness. After quickly looking at the trio by Claire's side, he pointed to a wheelchair parked near the admission desk. "Go grab that, will you? We'll get Taylor settled."

Claire hurried to do as Dr. Slattery bid, thinking that his calm, soothing voice was affecting her just the way she'd hoped her smile had reassured Deanna.

Too bad she didn't want her emotions around him calmed down. No, sir. She needed to be vigilant and on-call around this guy.

Claire wheeled the chair to the teen. He eased into it. Then, before Claire could stop her, Annie scrambled onto her brother's lap. "Hey, sweetie, you need to let your brother—"

In spite of his injury the boy made room for her, lifting his hand into the air so it wouldn't get jarred. "Don't worry, it's fine."

"No, it's not, Taylor," Deanna said, iron in her voice. "I'll take Annie while you get fixed up."

But the little girl cuddled closer.

Claire was just about to pry her away when Ty stopped her. "If we take a ride down the hall, then will you hop off?"

Amazingly, she nodded. Okay, maybe not so amazingly. Everyone—young and old—seemed to have a soft spot for Ty Slattery.

That's how the five of them ended up walking toward triage, all together, Ty in the lead, Claire pushing the chair and Deanna looking like she was in the middle of a really long streak of bad luck.

Claire knew that look. She had once been an overwhelmed young mom, too. More than a day or two had passed when she'd felt completely in over her head, but nobody had cared.

"Here we go," Dr. Slattery said, pushing through the stainless steel double doors. As soon as they stepped inside, he picked up the phone and spoke into it.

Claire did her best with the chair, the mother close to her heels. "I didn't mean for this to happen," Deanna said. "I never thought about Taylor getting cut."

"I know you didn't." Claire had never worried about broken glass or torn up cans either. She'd been too worried about feeding Wes. "That's why they're called *accidents,* right?"

The skin around her lips whitening, Deanna kept her focus on her son. "I suppose."

The teen closed his eyes. As Dr. Slattery spoke with two nurses, Deanna started looking agitated again. Seeking to calm her, Claire smiled. "So, how old is Annie?"

"Almost four."

"She's a cutie."

"Oh, she is. I tell you, more than one stranger's stopped me and said she needs to be on TV." After a pause, she added, "When I think of the things we've been going through, I can hardly believe it. I always thought I'd be doing better than this."

Reaching into her pocket, Claire wrote down two numbers. One was for the Applewood Women's Shelter, the other was her phone number at work. "This place helped me out a couple of years ago. You might want to give them a call. Or, call me if you like and we'll talk."

"You?"

Biting her lip, Claire nodded. "Yeah. I know exactly what you're going through. Applewood helped me a lot."

Further conversation was prevented by the appearance of the two nurses. "We'll take care of things now," one said as she reached for the wheelchair.

Deanna picked up Annie, who started crying. "I'm sorry," she said. "She just really likes being with Taylor."

"We'll be as quick as possible. I'll come get you after we take a look." With a genuine, warm smile, Ty said to Claire, "Thanks for your help. We'll handle this now. You'll make sure she gets the paperwork done?"

Thanks for her help? Oh, for heaven's sakes—she was just doing her job. "Yes, doctor."

Deanna stared at the curtained area all while juggling a squirming Annie in her arms. "I feel awful that I'm not in there with him."

"I know the feeling, but I promise, right now it would be better for Taylor if you and Annie let Dr. Slattery and the nurses do their jobs. They're good people, I promise."

"Do you know that doctor very well?"

"I do." Claire knew more about Ty Slattery than she wanted to. He was a resident, too handsome, too friendly and four years younger than herself. "Dr. Slattery's a good doctor."

After handing Deanna the paperwork again, Claire knew it was time to leave. "You take care, Ms. Johns," Claire murmured, barely waiting for her to reply before retreating to the safety of the reception area.

But as the double doors whooshed open and Claire stepped through, she didn't know if she was more anxious to put some space between her and Deanna Johns—a woman who reminded her way too much of her past—or the one man who'd reminded her that maybe she wasn't as dead inside as she'd previously thought.

"HEY, CLAIRE," Dr. Slattery called out just as she was heading out to the back parking lot.

Pulling her navy coat a little more tightly closed, Claire did her best to look relaxed. "Hi. Um, is Taylor okay?"

"I think so. Twelve stitches plus a tetanus shot." He chuckled. "He's going to have a sore hand for quite a while."

And more than likely would be sleeping in a car tonight, Claire realized. She should have thought to go back and see if Deanna had any questions about the shelter. She'd meant to, but had forgotten when she'd reached the main reception room. At least a dozen patients had come in while she'd been gone and Lynette's usual good temper was in short supply. They'd worked nonstop the next four hours.

But Dr. Slattery didn't need to know any of that. "Well, thanks again for helping us out."

"Like I said, I'm glad I hadn't left yet."

He was so laid-back and easygoing it was everything Claire could do to remember that she didn't want to lower her guard around him. His calm, caring demeanor reminded Claire that some men might actually be everything they claimed to be. That was always a nice surprise, since Ray, her ex-husband, hadn't been.

Dr. Slattery stepped closer, effectively making it difficult to forget that she needed to stay far away from him. "How's Wes?"

"Wes? Fine."

"Shoulder still doing okay?"

She remembered Dr. Slattery's hands gently working Wes's shoulder at a wrestling tournament a good month ago, checking to see if any real harm had been done on that mat. "It's in shape, if his performance is any indication. He won two wrestling matches last weekend."

A true smile lit his face. "I can't believe I was on call all weekend and didn't get to see a single match. I'll have to stop by and watch him compete one day soon."

"I'm sure you're too busy for that." When he blinked in surprise, Claire attempted to soften her words with a smile. "I mean, you're a resident, and help with the football conditioning at Lane's End High, too. You can't watch all the kids all the time, right?"

"I do my best." He eyed her again, then ran a hand through his dark brown hair. "Are you off duty now?"

"I am."

"I'm a little too keyed up to go home. Would you like a cup of coffee or something?"

"No." She bit her lip, then said, "I mean, thanks, but I've got to get home to Wes. He's probably already combing the cupboards for junk to eat."

He laughed. "He wouldn't be a teenage boy if he wasn't."

Relief rushed through her as she realized he wasn't going to make a big deal about her refusing him. "He's barely a teenager…only thirteen."

"I still find it hard to believe you have an eighth-grader."

"Yeah, well." No way was she going to discuss how she got pregnant too early, married the wrong guy for the wrong reasons, and then nearly lost Wes when her marriage and her financial situation fell apart.

Those days would probably seem like another world to such a handsome, successful guy. Correction, *young* guy. "Well. Good night, Dr. Slattery."

He flashed a smile. "Maybe we could graduate to first names? It's Ty."

Claire knew that she'd been hanging on to some kind of weird, outdated formality by insisting on using his title. She wanted to keep her distance. "All right. Ty." She smiled to take the sting out of her voice, though she doubted he even felt a pinch. "I better get on home."

"How about I walk you to your car? It's dark out here."

"Thanks, but that's not necessary."

He fell into step beside her. "It's the least I can do. I'm sure Wes would appreciate someone looking out for his mom."

Unfortunately, her son had already needed to find someone to look out for his mom. Never again would she be in a situation where she felt dependent or inferior. Never again did she want to depend on a man, even for safety's sake. "I'm okay."

"Even so…"

Slowly they walked through along rows of cars and finally stopped in front of her gold Corolla. She shivered a little at the cold, anxious to get in the car and head home. "This is me. Good night, Ty."

"For some reason, my schedule's a little bit lighter this week. Maybe we'll see each other around sometime soon. I'll try and make Wes's next match."

Even though Wes liked Ty, even though she knew the guy meant his offer innocently, Claire was in no hurry to make any plans with him. She was not in the market for a relationship. And if she was, it definitely wouldn't be with someone who made her forget all the reasons why she wasn't in the market in the first place.

But she didn't want to be rude. It wasn't Ty's fault she wasn't dating material. "Maybe so." As she turned on the ignition, Claire watched him stride past her parking area to the physician's lot.

As she pulled out, she saw him behind her, in an Jeep that also looked as if it had seen better days. That took her by surprise—she'd thought all medical residents drove cars at least a little bit nicer than that.

And as she turned left to go one way on the freeway, he went the other.

All served to remind her that there was more separating her and Dr. Ty Slattery than job titles and makes of automobiles.

She'd been widowed, then homeless. She'd collected cans, just like Deanna and Taylor had. She'd almost died and had stayed in the hospital nearly two weeks. Now she lived in a two-bedroom apartment, truly the worst housing in the best school district she could afford.

Ty Slattery had probably never even thought about the exact price of a McDonald's cheeseburger. She doubted he'd ever worried about his power getting turned off, had probably never been the recipient of pitied stares and too-concerned expressions.

Fumbling for her cell phone, she punched in her home phone number. "Wes, I'm on my way," she said the minute he answered.

"Good. I'm starved."

And with that, all Claire's troubles melted away. There was only one man in her life who mattered and he had size ten feet and was single-handedly trying to eat her out of house and home. "I'll bring home a pizza," she said with a smile. "A pizza big enough for two."

Chapter Two

"Ty, wait up," Chris Pickett called out just as Ty was paying for his groceries and about to head back out into the frosty parking lot.

Grabbing hold of his two sacks, Ty turned around and waited for his best friend from high school to wheel his loaded shopping cart over. "I can't believe we're seeing each other at the grocery store. Who would have ever thought back when we were seniors that we'd be here on a Friday night?"

"I promised Beth I'd pick up some dinner on the way home. She's been sick as a dog," Chris explained.

"Morning sickness all day long, huh?"

"Morning, noon and night. Doc, you said by the fifth month she was going to be feeling better."

"I told you I was the wrong person to ask. I've delivered babies but haven't helped out with too many pregnancies. Give her OB a call."

"Beth won't…she doesn't want to be a bother." Chris rested his elbows on the handrail of the cart. "That's why I'm grocery shopping at seven at night. What's your excuse?"

Ty stepped to the side so two bundled-up teenagers in Lane's End High black and gold hoodies could squeeze by. "I live alone. I either shop or don't eat."

"You're making things too difficult. You're supposed to be out at a club or something when you're single."

"Not if you've just spent the last twelve hours on call," Ty replied, thinking that his words didn't tell the half of it. "I ended up staying two hours later than I intended when a boy with a cut hand came in, followed by a dozen people with the flu."

"Ah, winter."

"Yeah." Ty also had no extra money for clubs or dates, but that was nothing Chris needed to know about.

"Too bad." Brightening, Chris said, "Hey, want to come over on Sunday and watch the football games?"

"Beth won't mind?"

"Nah. You always make her smile. Come on over for a free meal, Ty. There'll be plenty of food."

Ty raised an eyebrow at the comment. Hmm. Maybe his struggling financial situation wasn't too much of a secret after all. "Thanks. I'll double-check my hospital schedule then let you know."

"Call me either way. You spend too much time working as it is. You could use a little R & R."

"I'll call. I promise."

When Chris's cell phone started buzzing, Ty waved goodbye and strode out to his car. For a split second, he gave into feelings of jealousy. His buddy from high school had done everything "right." He'd gone to a nearby college, met Beth, then, after they'd both gradu-ated with business degrees, they had settled into good jobs and had been working their way up the corporate ladder ever since.

Now, after five years of marriage, they were expecting their first child, who was destined to live in a well-kept home and be driven around in some designer station wagon.

He, on the other hand, was trying to finish up his residency and find a job. He also worked when he could for Lane's End public schools. He helped coach and condition athletes so he could afford a meal out once in a while.

In the distance, Ty saw Chris pull out of the parking lot, still on his cell phone. Most likely, the guy was talking to Beth. Probably talking about that baby again. Ty tried to shrug off his melancholy.

Tiny, icy bits of snow started falling as he drove along the narrow, hilly streets of Lane's End. The flakes stuck to his windshield like glue. Ty turned the wipers to a higher speed and pressed the button for wiper spray.

In the distance, bells rang from the hundred-year-old steeple at the First Baptist Church. The bright chimes echoed through the streets, lending as much character and personality to Lane's End as the flowers hanging in baskets around the scenic historic district in the summer.

After catching a green light at the top of Mission Street, Ty finally pulled into his own house, a restored three bedroom home in the heart of downtown Lane's End that he rented from another doctor. The ancient oak door stuck as he worked the key into the lock, turning it first to the left, then firmly to the right. When he entered, the first real sense of peace washed over him as he carried his grocery sacks into the remodeled kitchen.

Home, at least for now. The ceilings were a little too low,

and the wooden floor was scratched and scraped from Maisy's toenails. A faint chill crawled out of the window frames and the kitchen faucet had a constant, slow drip. But even counting all those flaws, Ty loved the old place. He loved how it made him feel, living in a house that had been home to so many before him.

Ty wasn't sure why Dr. Michaels had offered him the place to rent for the past two years, but Ty was extremely grateful. Every two years, the elderly doctor offered one of the residents the home to live in for next to nothing. Dr. Michaels jokingly said it was his way of knowing that at least one of the residents was getting enough rest at night.

Ty knew it was a stroke of good luck. If he wasn't living on Mission Street, some days he thought he'd be living *in* a mission.

Now, he had a rundown place with lots of personality and a really nice kitchen, thanks to the previous resident who'd accidentally flooded the dishwasher and ruined the floor and cabinetry.

Quickly, Ty emptied his grocery bags, pulling out the boxes of Hungry-Man dinners that had been on sale, along with two boxes of cereal, a case of Ramen noodles, and a gallon of milk. After picking out the Salisbury steak dinner, Ty leaned back against the counter as the microwave did its magic.

Maisy hopped off the couch and finally came over to say hello.

"How are you doing, girl?" he asked his old retriever. "You keep everything running smooth today?"

Maisy lifted her muzzle so he could scratch her behind her ears. He let her outside and as Ty watched his old dog carefully make her way down the snow-covered back steps, he sipped a beer and thought about the woman he'd been trying so hard to ignore: Claire Grant.

From the moment he saw her hovering over her son at the wrestling meet, he'd been charmed. There was something so delicate about her…though he was quickly finding out that she was hardly fragile at all.

No, behind those wide-set golden eyes and dark blond hair was a woman who relied on herself. All practicality and patience.

He'd seen something in her son at the meets that reminded him of himself. He saw something in her manner that reminded him of the not-so-good places he'd been. He'd heard phrases he knew well. Words that didn't say much but effectively covered up not-so-good circumstances. He saw pretty smiles that never quite reached the eyes.

And one day, weeks ago, he'd heard her tell her coworker Lynette she was "fine." And that "fine" told him so much.

He should know—he'd had plenty of experience telling everyone he was fine when inside he was feeling like a lit match.

Those similarities had intrigued him. They made him want to get to know her better. And for a split second, he'd thought she felt the same way. But she'd rebuffed his clumsy offer of coffee.

He had enough of an ego to first be taken aback. He thought he looked pretty good, he had a good job. He was stable. All those things counted, right?

He'd thought they did.

So why had she said no? Was it really because of Wes?

Was it because she didn't date? Or, was it that she didn't want to date *him?*

Maisy's scratching at the door brought him back to the present. "Let's have some dinner, girl," he said, pouring a cupful of Mighty Munchies into her bowl.

As Maisy attacked her food with gusto, Ty made a mental note to visit Wes's next wrestling match. It wouldn't do any harm to check on the boy's shoulder. At the very least, Claire looked like she could use another friend. He supposed he could, too.

As the latest basketball results filled the TV screen, he almost felt happy. Maybe for once everything was going to work out.

HE FELT DIFFERENTLY at three in the morning. With a weary hand, Ty rubbed his eyes and moved to the edge of his bed, too-tense muscles once again warring with an active mind. Four hours tonight.

All in all, that was pretty good.

He didn't sleep. He hadn't since college, when he'd worked and studied at odd hours. Now, in his residency, sleep was a catch-can thing, too.

He just wished night demons wouldn't plague him all the while and make things worse. Because the night was when he remembered the heartbreak of Sharon.

And he could still remember exactly what she'd said. There was no way she wanted to be saddled with a guy who was going to owe more money than she could imagine making during the next couple of years. And, well, she'd met someone else. An older guy who'd just been hired on at a big investment firm. It was time to call it quits.

Ty didn't need a counselor to tell him that his mother's leaving, his father's lack of warm fuzzies and his girl-friend's betrayal was enough to deliver a whopper of a punch. For a lifetime.

And it had.

Oh, he'd gotten through it, it was what he did best— what he'd learned to do back when he was a kid and nobody was around to get him up in the morning.

You didn't complain. You did the best you could and tried to feel satisfied. You learned not to trust other people because sometimes things didn't work out the way you wanted them to.

But maybe it was time to do things a little differently. Maybe it was time to start living again.

Chapter Three

"Claire, I really appreciate you helping us out," Gene Davidson said from the doorway leading into the concession stand the following Saturday. "We were really short-handed for volunteers at today's meet."

"It's not a problem, coach," she replied, muscling the giant amount of pancake batter in the industrial-size bowl. Feeding almost a hundred wrestlers after weigh-ins required an amazing amount of pancakes! "I'm a team parent. We all have to help out sooner or later."

"Wes told me you've been putting in a lot of hours at the hospital. I bet you'd rather be sleeping at six-thirty on a Saturday morning."

Claire wondered why Gene even brought that up. She was pretty sure all the parents on the team worked hard and would rather be sleeping in.

"Wes has to be here anyway," she said with a smile. "Don't worry about me."

Gene held up a hand. "I'm not worried, I just wanted you to know I appreciate your time."

Claire's shoulders relaxed as she realized she wasn't

going to have to go to battle with the man to prove once again that she was stronger than she looked.

As yet another rush of boys passed, their hair sticking straight up and sleepy expressions on their faces, Claire stopped stirring for a moment and tried to find Wes.

He'd been grumpy this morning, answering all her questions with one-word answers. Claire wondered if he was more nervous about the meet than he let on.

Unfortunately, Claire didn't see a hint of her son in the crowd of teenagers. Only a familiar man leaning against the wall near the kitchen entrance and checking off something on a clipboard.

Ty Slattery smiled when their eyes met. "Way to put Coach Davidson in his place," he said, making it obvious he'd heard every word of her previous conversation. "I bet he won't say a word next time you show up early to make pancakes."

Oops. "Did I sound rude?"

"Not rude, just a little brusque." Stepping forward, he said, "How are you this morning?"

"I'm fine."

"Glad to hear it."

The look Ty gave her, so warm and caring, made Claire stir the batter with a little more force than necessary. Made her think maybe he was more attractive than she'd originally thought.

His look made Claire feel like she was missing something. Made her remember that once upon a time she believed in dreams and fairy tales. In happily-ever-afters.

No way was she ever going down that path again. "You're here early, too."

"I'm working today—helping to coach and with any medical emergencies."

"Gene should have been thanking you for your time. I know you've been putting in long hours at the hospital—practically every time I've come in your name has been listed as one of the doctors on duty."

He shrugged off her comment. "It's part of being a resident, I guess. Fortunately, this last rotation of mine is not too intense. I've got more days and weekends off than I can ever remember having."

More kids wandered by. Jill Young, another wrestling parent, reached behind her to get cooking spray. "I'll get started on the griddle, Claire."

Claire was just about to say her goodbyes to Ty when he spoke again. "Coach asked if I'd check out a couple of kids for Lane's End and the other competing teams. I decided to catch them while they weighed in. I'll be sure and take a good look at Wes's shoulder."

"Thanks. I appreciate that."

Because he was still standing there—even though they'd both commented on how busy they were and how much there still was to do—she said, "You can come back for pancakes when you're done."

"Are you finally agreeing to have a meal with me, Claire?"

"I'm offering to make you some pancakes, Dr. Slattery."

After almost a full minute, Ty replied. "I'll take you up on that. Beggars and choosers, you know."

Just like she'd touched a barbed wire, a little zing charged right through her when he smiled again before turning to another group of incoming boys.

With more care than necessary, Claire picked up the

whisk and attacked the batter again. No. She so did not need to even think about Ty Slattery…or her reaction to him.

Surely there had to be something about him she didn't like. His smile? No, she liked that fine. The way he looked in those baggy khakis, like he'd rolled out of bed into the first pair of trousers that were available? No, rumbled clothes had never bothered her.

Maybe she really didn't like the way he was always around. Always so helpful, like she didn't have a mind of her own. Maybe it was his playful semi-flirting.

Yeah. That's what she didn't like. She didn't like that one bit.

Claire, you're worthless! Ray's voice charged forth from the dead. Reminding her that she didn't need—or want—a man in her life.

She might make pancakes for men. She might even serve them with a smile. But she sure as heck didn't need to have them flirting with her. No way. No how.

"You okay, Claire? I think the batter's called a truce," Jill said.

With a clatter, the spoon hit the side of the stainless steel bowl. "Sorry, I don't know where my mind went. I think I'll go check on the syrup."

Claire scurried out before Jill could say a word about that.

FIVE HOURS LATER, Wes slipped a burnished pewter-colored medal around his neck. "It's only fourth place, Mom," he said modestly, though his eyes told a whole different story. In them, Claire saw triumph and pride, two things that she knew were hard to obtain.

"Fourth place is terrific! We'll have to put that medal on the wall at home."

Wes looked over at the boy from a neighboring district wearing the gold medal. "It's not that big a deal."

His hot and cold bursts were wearing her out. "I think it is. If they didn't think fourth place was special, they wouldn't have made a medal for it, now would they?"

His chin rose and, in his eyes, a faint glimmer of pride shone for a moment. "I never thought of that."

Unable to stop herself from touching him, Claire brushed back a thatch of hair from his forehead. "That's why you have me, honey. To remind you."

Like a flash, her son's expression changed again. "Mom!"

"What?"

"Don't call me that," he whispered. "And don't do that, either."

Claire felt like she'd just been slapped. "Don't do what?" For the life of her, all she could remember doing was being encouraging. "Wes, I'm just trying—"

"Stop, Mom."

As Wes ran off to the locker room to wash as well as he could and get changed, Claire sat back down, letting her shoulders slump in the near empty stands.

"You okay?"

Ty. For once, she didn't even care that he was nearby. Again. Right that minute, she could use a friend. Any friend. Correction, any understanding person. "Yeah."

"You don't look like it."

Resting her elbows on her thighs, Claire said, "It's nothing. Just teenage boy stuff. It's all new to me."

"What? You weren't a teenage boy once?"

That made her laugh. "You're right. I never thought I'd say this, but this is when I miss having a brother. I seem to really be messing up this afternoon."

As boys and parents wandered around, picking up old Gatorade bottles, sweatpants and smelly socks, Claire kept her attention on the locker room door.

Ty kept his attention on Claire. He knew she was a single mom, but didn't know much about her past. He also couldn't help but notice that she didn't mention Wes's dad. Giving in to impulse, he said, "Where is Wes's dad?"

Her eyes became guarded again. "Gone."

"Oh." Yep, that question had been a mistake. "Sorry. It's none of my business."

"Don't worry about it. It's no secret." Finally sparing him a glance, Claire shrugged and added, "He passed away about three years ago."

"I'm sorry."

"It's okay. We were separated before that. We had a lot of problems. He, um, wasn't a good husband. But he did love Wes. In his own way, at least. I guess that counts for something, huh?"

Thinking back to his own childhood, where his dad did the best he could even though a lot of times it wasn't too good at all, Ty nodded.

Claire tucked a strand of hair behind her ear and smiled weakly. "Sorry, I'm not one of those people who loves to talk about themselves."

He got that. He didn't like to talk about himself, either.

And because her announcement was so refreshing, sounded so good, he wanted to know more. What had happened with her husband? He hadn't been *a good husband?* What did that mean? What had happened to her?

Since she obviously didn't want to speak of it, he gestured to the boys' locker room. "What set Wes off?"

"I praised fourth place and called him 'honey.'" Biting her bottom lip, Claire said, "At least I think that's what I did wrong."

"Not so good to a competitive, tough wrestler. Almost fighting words."

Surprise and a bit of humor filled her gaze. "You get it."

"Unlike you, I was a boy once."

As they watched Wes, dressed in gray sweats and carrying an old backpack on his shoulder, leave the locker room with two other boys, Ty noticed a ribbon around the boy's neck, though the medal was tucked under his sweatshirt. "Something tells me he's prouder of that medal than he let on."

"You think so?" Hope sprang to life in her eyes. "When I said that I thought fourth place was great, he glared. I keep saying the wrong things today."

"Ever think that maybe you're saying everything right and it's Wes who's taking everything wrong?"

"No. I need to support Wes. To be the best person I possibly can for him. I'll just have to work on my words with him a little bit more."

Wes picked up his pace as he approached. "Hi, Dr. Slattery."

"Hi."

Wes looked at him curiously. Claire probably would never see it, but there was a definite look of possession in the boy's posture. Wes put it into words. "What are you doing here with my mom? My shoulder was good today."

"It looked like it. I just wanted to tell you I saw your pin in that last match. How many seconds did that last? Thirty?"

"Coach said twenty-eight."

There was a hint of a swagger in Wes's voice. Ty firmly kept his expression low-key instead of smiling. "Impressive."

"Yeah. I'm not very good. Some guys on the squad did youth wrestling, so they've got lots of experience. I'm getting better, though."

"Good enough to place, huh?"

Wes fingered the ribbon around his neck. "Yeah. I was really surprised. This is just my second year. Coach said I did a good job."

Though Claire was quiet, Ty noticed she was loving the amount of information Wes was divulging. Obviously, the boy had mastered the "I'm fine, nothing's new" routine. Because he was intrigued by Claire's past and because it looked like Wes could use a buddy, he impulsively said, "Hey, I was thinking about going out for chili. Are you hungry, Wes? Maybe we could all grab something to eat."

"I'm starved." After glancing his mom's way, he tempered his response. "I mean, yeah, I could probably eat."

Now all Ty had to do was convince Wes's mom to give him a chance. "Do you like Cincinnati chili, Claire?"

She blinked. "Not really."

"Oh. Well, they have other things at Skyline," he said quickly. Why hadn't he offered to go out for burgers? "I think they have salads there."

"Thanks, but I don't think—"

"It's just food, Claire. I promise."

"Thanks, but maybe some other time." Turning to her son, she said, "Wes, are you ready to go home?"

Wes hadn't moved. "No. I'm starving, Mom. Why can't we go out to eat? We never go out to eat."

Something dimmed in her eyes. "That's because—"

Quickly Ty spoke. The last thing he'd wanted to happen was to bring up a touchy subject. "You sure about dinner? We could go to Wendy's or something—"

After another look at Wes, Claire said, "You know what? Chili's fine."

"So that means we can go?" Wes asked.

"I think fourth place deserves a special treat." Hesitantly, she glanced Ty's way. "Are you sure you have time to eat with us, Dr. Slattery?"

Wes rolled his eyes. "Mom, he asked us."

"I wouldn't have asked if I didn't want your company," Ty stressed.

"Please, Mom?"

"All right, then. We'll meet you there. For chili."

"Great. I'll go ahead and get us a table." Ty walked out before Claire could change her mind.

Of course, Ty didn't know if Claire had ultimately agreed because she, too, knew there was something tangible between them…or if she was only thinking of her son.

At the moment, he didn't want to know.

Chapter Four

After edging her Corolla out of the icy parking lot and onto the salt-treated streets, Claire sneaked a peek at Wes.

Without a word, he'd tossed his backpack on the backseat and climbed in next to her. Now he was pushing buttons on the radio, flipping stations every twenty seconds. With each push, clips of loud music burst out of the speakers, jarring Claire even more than the chunks of gravel and snow under the wheels of the car. "Choose a station *now*, Wes."

"I'm trying."

"Choose or the radio's going off," she said, purposely injecting a tone that welcomed no argument.

His finger hovered over the knob before he defiantly turned it off himself. "Fine. Now nothing's on. Happy?"

Claire bit back a sigh as she slowly rolled to a stop at the light. What in the world was going on with him? Was this typical teen behavior? Something more?

Instead of berating him for his attitude, she cast him a worried look. "What's wrong? You okay?"

"I guess."

Something *was* wrong. That gravelly tone in his voice only came when he was on the verge of tears. "Listen, I'm sorry I snapped about the radio, but it's hard to concentrate on the road when a different song clicks on every two seconds. You'll understand when you're driving."

"That's a long time from now."

"Not so long. Just three years."

"That's forever."

As the light turned green and she accelerated, Claire privately knew better. Forever was never a long time.

For years, it had just been the two of them. Wes probably didn't realize it, but he was her stability, her rock. No matter what was going on in their lives, she could count on Wes to be her partner. Now it looked like that relationship was changing.

"You can try the radio again if you want."

After a moment's pause, Wes pushed the button and again went through the whole process, just like he hadn't heard a word she said. As Christina got replaced by Pink and then by some rapper, Claire had had enough. Pushing the power button in, an abrupt silence permeated the interior of the car.

Wes scowled. "What did you do that for?"

"You know why. You pushing button after button gives me a headache."

"There's no good music on."

"I told you we could pop in a cassette."

"Mom, your car has to be the only one in Ohio that still has a cassette player. We need a CD player. Or better yet, an iPod. You can get an attachment so you can hear your iPod in the car."

So much for Wes being her partner. If he was, he'd realize she was pretty darn happy to have a car, an apartment, food and money in the bank. "Maybe next year."

"It's always next year."

"We used to hope for the very things we have now," she pointed out, just about at the end of her patience. "I'm surprised you've forgotten what life was like, living in our van."

He slumped. "I haven't forgotten. I just get sick of never having what everyone else has. Here in Lane's End everyone has stuff I don't."

"Even rich kids want things they don't have, Wes. You need to learn to be happy with what you've got. Count your blessings."

"You tell me that every day."

"Obviously I need to. What is going on with you? Is it the wrestling meet? Is your shoulder bothering you?"

"No."

"What? And don't say *nothing*. We're almost at Skyline Chili. I don't want you pulling this attitude in front of Dr. Slattery—especially since he was nice enough to ask us out to eat."

His eyes narrowed. "How come he invited us, anyway? How come Dr. Slattery is always talking to you?"

Well, there it was. Wes was wondering what was going on with Ty and herself. And since she didn't really know, Claire decided to slowly feel her way through the conversation. "I didn't realize Ty was *always* talking to me."

"Mom, he sat near you when he ate pancakes. I saw. Now he wants us to go out for chili with him."

"Why are you asking me about this now? You're the one who wanted to go out to eat. I tried to go home. Remember?"

"I remember. It's just that we never go out to eat."

"You know the reason for that. So, you only wanted to go out because it's a restaurant meal?"

"Maybe I like talking to Dr. Slattery sometimes. He's pretty cool. For someone so old."

Claire curbed a smile. The way Wes spoke, it sounded like Ty was ancient. And she definitely knew her son liked being around men and doing "guy" stuff. Maybe this meal wasn't such a bad idea, after all. Choosing her words carefully, Claire said, "You know, Ty is pretty cool. And going out to eat during the week is pretty special. Maybe he feels the same way. Dr. Slattery lives alone, you know."

The conversation paused as Claire slowly turned right, then left. There weren't too many cars on the street, which was a real blessing. The little Corolla did okay in bad weather but was no match against the powerful SUVs that seemed to be the norm in Lane's End.

Like Wes, sometimes she found herself wishing for things she didn't have.

Wes broke the silence just as the bright blue and yellow Skyline Chili sign loomed about a hundred yards away. "So. Do you like him?"

"I like Dr. Slattery fine."

"I mean like a boyfriend."

The question was as jarring as the mishmash of rock tunes had been. "No. I don't want a boyfriend."

"Why not?"

"Because I've already been married. Once was enough for me."

"He's probably rich. Doctors always are."

"It doesn't matter if he's rich or not. We're joining him

for *dinner,* not a future," she attempted to explain as finally—*finally*—they pulled into the parking lot and parked. "There is a difference."

"I know that. But, if you did date him, I wouldn't care. Very much."

What would he not care about? That she was dating? That it was Ty? That he was rich? "Thank you for that."

The car was still running. Conscious of the price of gasoline, she turned off the engine but made no move to get out.

Claire had a feeling that Ty was looking out the window and wondering why they hadn't just unbuckled and gone on in. But this was important. Hesitantly, she said, "Do you want to talk about things?"

"There's nothing to talk about."

That almost made her laugh. As far as Claire was concerned, they had everything to talk about! "Everything changes, Wes. You're growing up and becoming more independent. I'm working hard and learning to be independent, too. I guess it's no longer just the two of us against the world."

"When we were in the shelter—we had Tessa and Keaton."

Thinking of Tessa, who'd helped her so much while she'd been in the hospital and Keaton Phillips, the cop her friend had married, Claire said softly, "We still have them. You stay with them one weekend a month still."

"I like my visits with them."

"Do you want to see them more often?" Claire's heart broke, wondering if she was ever going to be good enough for her son.

"No." His hand on the door, he turned to her. "I'm sorry I said all that about the radio."

"I know. I'm sorry we don't have a CD player."

Twin splotches of color stained his cheeks. "I shouldn't have said that, either."

"It's okay to want things, honey. I want things, too."

"I'm saving for an iPod."

"That's good. I'm saving for a new couch. But while I'm looking forward to everything I want, I think I'm going to go enjoy a dinner out with a man who wants to be our friend. Sound like a plan?"

"Yeah."

"Okay, then. Let's not keep him waiting any longer. He'll think we stood him up."

Wes's eyes widened. Before Claire had even put the keys in her purse, he'd scrambled out of the car, hopped up on the sidewalk and run into the restaurant.

She followed at a much slower pace.

TY AND WES were already diligently reading menus when she arrived in the seating area after taking a quick trip to the ladies' room to wash her hands. To her surprise, he stood up when she arrived at the table.

Wes narrowed his eyes. "What'd you do that for?"

"You stand up when a woman comes to the table," Ty answered. "It's good manners."

"Oh." After a moment, Wes said, "Where'd you learn that?"

"My coach in high school. He was a stickler for things like standing up and saying *yes, ma'am.*"

"Mom's never made me say *ma'am.* She's never made me stand up for her, either."

With a wink in her direction, Ty said, "You don't stand

up because a lady asks you to. You stand up because it's the right thing to do." As he scooted back in his chair, he added, "Don't worry, Wes. You'll get the hang of it all and, if you don't, more people will step in to tell you what to do. My wrestling coaches in college spent hours giving me advice about how to get along in life."

Wes's eyes widened with a new respect. "You wrestled in college? I didn't know that."

Claire hadn't known that, either.

"Yep. I went to school on a wrestling scholarship. No one set up any college fund for me growing up."

There was more than a trace of bitterness in Ty's voice. Wes must have caught it, too, because he said, "Was college wrestling hard?"

"Yep. But, that was okay. Working hard has never been an issue for me. I had big dreams and I found a way to pay for them. That was lucky."

Claire liked Ty's spin on life. That he was lucky to be hardworking and goal-oriented. How many people looked at things from the complete opposite view point? Like they deserved more than they had?

Wes shifted in his seat, a sure sign that he was interested. "So that's why you go to so many wrestling meets. Because you used to wrestle."

"Partly," Ty replied, sending a shuttered look her way.

Claire received that look with some trepidation. What was he really saying? That he came to the meets to see her?

That made her uncomfortable.

Oh, not because he found her attractive. No, what made her uncomfortable was that she liked his interest. She swallowed hard, hoping to calm the knot in her stomach.

She needed to get a grip on herself, pronto! There was nothing romantic between them. And there couldn't be, ever.

After ordering sodas, cheese Coneys and 5-way spaghetti dinners all around, Wes saw a buddy of his. He bummed two dollars off Claire then joined his friend at the video arcade until the food arrived.

"Are you ever going to take off that coat?" Ty asked.

Quickly, she shrugged it off. "Sorry. I don't know where my mind is tonight." But she did. It was revolving around Ty, her attraction to him and the multitude of warning signals that were going off…reminding her that he was Mr. Unsuitable. Correction—Dr. Unsuitable. He was too young, too polished and too rich.

But he still had a great demeanor. He smiled, warming her insides. "Don't apologize for a thing, Claire. I just hoped you'd get comfortable around me. That's all."

Their sodas came. Claire sipped her root beer gratefully as she tried to think of something to say. Finally, she settled on their jobs. "How does your schedule work? Are you in the hospital all week?"

"I'm with a private physician one day a week, then spend the rest of the time in the emergency room at the hospital."

"And then you'll be up at the high school, working with the kids?"

"When I can." He shrugged off his crazy schedule like it was no big deal. "What about you?"

"Oh, I have pretty much the same schedule every day. On most days I work from eight to three. On Wednesdays I go in early and leave around noon."

"Then you're off to your other job, huh?"

He'd lost her. "What do you mean?"

"Being a mom?"

Glancing in her son's direction, Claire couldn't help but smile. "Yes. Lately, that's been just as challenging."

"If you handle motherhood like Deanna, I'd say you're doing all right. I had a chance to visit with her after I got Taylor patched up. She's a nice lady who really cares about her kids."

"I agree." Remembering Deanna and the tumble of emotions that the woman brought forth, Claire shook her head. "I hope they'll be okay. I gave her the name of a shelter."

"She mentioned that. If I had to guess, I'd say her luck was about to change."

"Why do you say that?"

"I don't know. Something tells me there's more to her than meets the eye. Some people are kind of like my house, a little rundown, but inside, they're in pretty good shape."

Claire laughed at the analogy. "Your place is like that, doctor? And here I thought you'd have a manicured lawn and organized cupboards."

"That's not me at all. I have very little in my cupboards, which is a good thing, because Maisy would probably find a way to get into them and chew everything in sight."

Wes joined them right at that minute. "Who's Maisy?"

"My dog. She's an old golden retriever."

"I love dogs," Wes said. Over his head, Claire shared a smile with Ty. Wes's dream had always been to have a dog of his own.

"Maybe one day you'll get a chance to meet her," Ty said offhandedly. "If you two do get the chance to meet, I'm sure the feeling will be mutual. Maisy loves everyone."

Their chili came. Claire picked at hers. She'd never been

one to totally love the chili-spaghetti-cheese-and-onion combo that everyone else in the city seemed to crave. Of course, it didn't really matter what was on her plate, anyway. The reason she was at Skyline was to make Wes happy.

With a lump in her throat, Claire realized Wes was having the time of his life. He really liked being around Ty. And Ty, for his part, seemed to know all the right things to say to her son.

She couldn't help but notice how skillfully Ty guided the conversation with Wes, discussing dogs and wrestling and video games with an ease she never had.

After a half hour of conversation, the check came. She'd just pulled out a twenty when Ty stood up to go pay at the counter. "Put that away. This is my treat."

"I can pay our way."

"It's just chili. You can pay next time."

Claire was just about to fumble her way through—not being sure there was going to be a next time—when Wes spoke up. "Mom likes to cook."

Ty's blue eyes issued a challenge. "How about you invite me over for dinner someday?"

Claire didn't trust herself to reply. She was afraid if she opened her mouth, she'd do something stupid, like actually offer an invitation. The next thing she knew, she'd be thinking about a real date with Ty. And that would be a huge mistake.

Unfortunately, her son had no such reservations. "How about next Saturday night?"

Claire's stomach rolled as Ty grinned. "How about next Saturday night, Claire? Would you like to have dinner together then?"

She glanced at Wes. Once again, she saw hope in his eyes. He liked Ty—he liked him a lot. And, well, she couldn't buy him iPods or new furniture, but she could cook Ty dinner, right?

True desperation engulfed her, making her feel anxious and...excited? "Sure. Why not? Next Saturday night would be fine."

Chapter Five

"Girl, you've got a date with a doc-tor," Lynette sang to Claire when the waiting room was empty for the first time since they'd started their shift.

"He's a resident."

"Shoot, that counts! You just raised yourself a good two feet, in my estimation." She paused, looking Claire over with her famous dark-as-night eyes. "Or just lowered yourself into my black book. Everyone knows doctors are egotistical jerks."

Everyone who knew Lynette Brown knew that her "black book" was the opposite of the proverbial bachelor's. Inside her book were lists of people she didn't care to associate with.

Well, so she said.

"Yep, as soon as I get out my pen, I'm going to have to hover it over the Gs and once again weigh the pros and cons of your clearheaded thinking." Pursing her lips, she added, "Or lack thereof."

Claire didn't know whether to burst out laughing or to hit Lynette with the file folder she was carrying. She settled for doing her best to maintain dignity. One of them had to do that, after all. "Stop."

"No way! This is the most exciting thing I've heard about since Jobeth over in radiology announced she was having twins!"

Jobeth's news had been good. This news was…strange. "Let's just drop it, can we?"

"Not on your life."

"Now I'm sorry I told you."

"I'm not." Waggling her freshly waxed eyebrows, Lynette whispered, "What else you got going in that top-secret life of yours? You inherit a bunch of money, too?"

"My life's not top secret."

"It feels that way. You never give me any news."

That was because there wasn't any news to tell. Usually, she liked it that way, too.

Claire couldn't even joke about her situation. From the moment she'd said yes last Saturday night she'd felt like she was teetering on the edge of a cliff, just one more misstep and she'd fall through the air. It was only because Ty was coming over the following evening—tomorrow night!—that she'd broken her normal code of silence.

Which had not been a good idea. Lynette's ribbing had been constant and full of mischief.

"I don't want to talk about this anymore. Forget I even told you."

"No way. This is the first time I've ever heard you knew people of the opposite sex. Most days, you never even notice when a man comes waltzing in our double doors."

"I'm not that bad."

"Pretty close." Glancing toward the doors fondly, Lynette murmured, "Remember Hunk-O-Man?"

"Oh, for heaven's sakes. Not Hunk-O-Man again."

"Why not? He was the most gorgeous thing I've seen in this Petri dish of a waiting room. Blond, blue-eyed, tan. Tall. Cover-model worthy."

Claire had to admit Hunk-O-Man had been memorable. Especially since he'd only come in with a jammed thumb—nothing infectious. And when they'd found out he'd hurt himself while climbing onto his neighbor's roof to fix a broken shingle, he'd gone down in waiting-room history as Lynette's model of the perfect man. Rugged and thoughtful.

Still talking, Lynette said, "I thought we were pretty close, but I've never, ever heard you talk about going on a date."

"That's because I don't date. I'm a widow, remember?"

"Well, I'm just glad you're doing something. Finally. And if it has to be with Dr. Ty I'm-handsome-as-sin Slattery, so be it."

Claire was saved from a reply by the arrival of an elderly couple sick with the flu and a teenager who'd cut his knees in a bike accident. Dutifully, she escorted them to a semi-private cubicle and took down their vital information.

But in between, she kept thinking back to the heart of what Lynette had been saying. *Why now? Why Ty?*

Claire could come up with a million reasons she said yes, all having to do with Wes. Still feeling residual guilt for everything she'd put him through when they'd been living on the streets, Claire knew she'd do everything within her power to give Wes what he wanted.

Well, everything within reason.

Had she only said yes because the dinner invitation had been the first thing that sparked life into his eyes during his current grumpy phase?

Maybe.

Or maybe she, too, had a soft spot for Ty. And dinner was *dinner*…not romance and flowers.

"Ty's nice," she told Lynette when they were once again standing behind the counter.

As if sensing she'd teased enough, Lynette squeezed her hand. "I'm glad. Nice is good."

"We're just friends, you know. Ty knows Wes from wrestling. In fact, Wes is the one who invited him over." Claire fought to maintain her look of innocence. Yep, that was Claire Grant, always putting her boy's needs first.

Lynette's lips twitched. "Well, I'm glad he did."

Claire's stomach was so jumpy, she couldn't honestly say the same thing. In fact, as the hours to the big dinner marched closer, she was sure it all was a very bad idea.

Really bad.

Especially since they hadn't discussed any details since their dinner at Skyline. She hadn't seen Ty more than from a distance all week. He hadn't called her, either. Maybe she'd just imagined they had dinner plans?

Then, just when she was sure she'd made too much out of *We ought to have dinner together on Saturday night,* there he was, waiting for her at the end of her shift. "Ty. Hi."

He smiled right back. "Hi. Hey, Lynette."

"Dr. Slattery." Lynette pressed a palm behind Claire's back and pushed her forward.

Claire moved out from behind the reception desk and a whole lot closer to Ty. "Is, uh, anything wrong?"

"No. I just thought I'd walk you out to your car. It's dark out."

Feeling like she was back in high school, Claire sneaked a peek at Lynette before walking to his side. Lynette gave a little wave in response.

Then he was taking her coat from her vise grip and helping her put it on. "Thanks." Summoning up something to say, she said, "Listen, I'm so glad you're here. We probably ought to talk about—"

He interrupted. "Hold on, let me make sure I heard that right. You're glad to see me?"

She rolled her eyes. She was cooking him a meal for Wes. So he could have a man's company. Not because she wanted to be around Ty. "I was going to say that I needed to give you directions to my house. And, uh, do you like pasta?"

He smiled. "I like everything."

"I have a recipe for baked ziti. It's nothing fancy, but—"

"I meant it when I said I like everything," he said quietly. Slow, like she needed extra time to process his words. And maybe she did. Claire noticed she got suspiciously tongue-tied whenever he was nearby. "I'm sure whatever you make will be great."

"All right, then." Breathe deep, she cautioned herself. Don't think of anything except right now. Unbidden, advice from a counselor flashed clear as day, like a photographer had just stepped into her life and carefully documented a moment in time. *Concentrate on today.*

Claire supposed Ty's proximity was making her feel the same way that she used to—flustered. Uncertain. In fact, when he'd halted her dinner talk by resting one hand on her arm, she'd flinched—a knee-jerk reaction to a man's touch.

He noticed. Just as quickly, he pulled his hand away, an expression crossing his face that Claire knew had everything to do with caution and care.

As the murky glow of the parking-lot light shone upon them and the topic of dinner and what to serve had been exhausted, Claire tried to cover up the burst of tension she felt whenever she was near him. "Looks like snow again."

Very systematically, Ty placed both hands behind his back. Showing her that he wasn't going to touch her again without her consent.

Making her realize he knew more about her than she'd thought.

"It sure does look like snow," he murmured.

Frustrated with herself, with her body's reaction to sudden touches—thanks to one randomly violent ex-husband—Claire deposited her tote bag on the hood of her car and hastily pulled out a pen and paper.

"My place is easy to get to from here," she said, unable to bring herself to discussing her flinching. Of course, what could she say? That she was holding on to a bag of past experiences so tightly that it was a wonder she could ever loosen her grip? "Do you know Lane's End very well?"

"Pretty well. I live here, too."

Why didn't she know that? She'd just assumed he lived farther into Cincinnati. In expensive Hyde Park or one of the more trendy places where up-and-coming singles lived. "I'm in the Arrowlake Apartments."

"Off Main?"

"Yep."

She wrote down quick directions even as she said them out loud. "If you go in the second entrance, we're the far back building…F. Wes and I are on the second floor. Apt. 210F."

"What time?"

"Seven?"

"Seven's just fine. I'll see you and Wes tomorrow night at seven o'clock."

Their fingers touched when the note was passed. For the first time, though, Ty didn't look attentive, only troubled. "Would you like me to bring anything?"

"No, it's my treat, remember?"

"A bottle of wine? Do you like wine?"

"That sounds nice." She attempted to smile, finding the transition in their conversation unnerving. "I like red."

"Red it is. Bye, Claire." He stepped away, but did pause to see that she'd unlocked her car door and that it started up just fine.

As Claire drove out of the parking lot under his watchful eye, she wondered what he was thinking. Dismay that she was obviously damaged goods? Wondering how he was going to neatly get himself out of her life? Out of Wes's life?

Then what would she do? Wes really liked Ty.

A trickle of cold sweat snaked down her back. Oh, why had she ever said yes to chili?

Why had she ever been remotely attracted to him?

SATURDAY AFTERNOONS were for transcribing notes from the week's cases. Folder after folder, Ty furiously worked, double-checking his notes and the course of action.

Making sure he'd followed through on requests for follow-ups, X-rays and phone calls.

As usual, it took three times as long as he hoped and today was even longer. But there was no hurry, the snow that Claire had predicted had begun to fall and hadn't let up in the last eight hours. Weather reports confirmed that everything was just going to get worse—an ice storm was headed in.

On the TV screen, listings of cancelled Sunday church services were already starting to show up. New weather reports cautioned everyone to stay off the roads if at all possible.

Though Ty had no qualms about driving in the snow—he'd gone to college in Michigan and it would take a whole lot more snow than seven inches to worry him—he was glad he had spent the day working on his home computer instead of on the roads.

Hours later, he'd just pressed save when the power flickered, then shut off. With a squawk, the emergency radio clicked on and, two minutes later, Ty heard the problem. The anticipated ice had indeed come. And that icy precipitation had pulled down a bunch of power lines.

"Maisy, it looks like we're going to be living in the dark for a while."

Maisy wagged her tail, then flopped to her side.

Then his cell phone rang. Looking at the glowing readout, he smiled. "Hey, Claire."

"Our power just went out."

"It's out here, too."

"Wes and I just heard that it's going to be a while."

"I heard that, too." After closing the lid of his laptop, he stood up. There was worry in Claire's voice. "Are you okay?"

"Actually…no. I'm afraid we're going to have to postpone our dinner invitation. I can't very well make you pasta without power."

"Sandwiches are fine, but I understand."

"There's more. With the power out, there's no heat. It's going to be pretty cold. I don't want to freeze you."

The temperature was sure to fall steadily at his place, too, though his wood-burning fireplace would keep things good. "Do you have a fireplace?"

"No."

"I do."

She paused. "Well, I'm glad…."

"I didn't mean it how it sounded." Had she really thought he was bragging like a seven-year-old? "I meant, how about you and Wes come over here for the evening?"

"No. I mean, thank you, but we couldn't impose."

"You're not imposing, I offered."

"That's very kind of you, but we'll be fine. So, maybe another—"

He interrupted fast before she hung up. "Claire, I'd still like your company…I have two guest bedrooms. If the power doesn't come on you can stay in one of them or we could all camp out in front of the fireplace."

"No! Really, we couldn't spend the—oh, hold on." Ty heard her not too successfully discuss his offer with Wes. After another minute, she got back on the line, her voice more harried than usual. "Thanks again. Bye."

Ty clicked off but stared at the receiver. For about the thirtieth time, he wondered what had happened to Claire Grant to make her so cautious and frightened.

Who had given her reason to flinch from a man's touch?

To not ask for anything? To only accept favors when they were geared toward her son?

After another five minutes, he decided to call her back. He wanted to see her, and he wanted to see her warm. Luckily, his buddy Wes answered. "Hi, Dr. Slattery," he said. "What's going on?"

"I called to try to talk you two into coming over here," Ty explained, only feeling slightly guilty for going behind Claire's back. "I've got a fireplace and a whole lot of sleeping bags. We can make a fire and cook hotdogs. What do you think?"

After a significant pause, Wes blurted, "We can't. My mom says you're only offering because you're being nice."

"I am being nice, but I want the company, too. After all, we did have plans, didn't we?"

"Hold on," Wes said and, before Ty could give him any hints on how to approach Claire with his offer, Ty heard him yell out, "Mom, Dr. Slattery's on the phone!"

Wes also couldn't muffle Claire's response. "Wesley Grant! Did you call him?"

"No. He called," Wes replied. "Mom, he really wants us to come over."

Ty couldn't resist grinning.

"Even if we wanted to go to his house, our car couldn't make it."

Wes got back on the phone. "Did you hear that?"

"Oh, yeah. Tell your mom that I can get there in fifteen minutes and to pack two bags. Y'all are coming over until the power comes back on."

For the first time, a hint of amusement lingered in Wes's voice. "Mom doesn't like being told what to do."

"I don't, either."

To Ty's relief, Wes laughed. "Hold on again." After the static muffling of his hand slapping on the receiver, Wes called out, "We're supposed to pack two bags."

"I don't think—"

"Mom, are you going to talk to Dr. Slattery or not?"

The phone clanked on a table. After a bit of shuffling, Claire got back on the line. "What are you doing, calling my son and informing us to get bags packed?"

She sounded mad enough to spit. "I'm being an egotistical chauvinist pig. I'm admitting it. But that doesn't stop my offer from being genuine."

As he'd hoped, her voice softened. "Oh."

"Are you really going to ruin a perfectly good offer because of your pride? The news said the power's out all over the city. Crews won't be able to get to residential areas for at least another twelve hours. If you don't come sit by my fire, you and your boy are going to get really cold."

She paused. "I'll pack a bag. Thank you."

After she'd clicked off, Ty looked around the room. Dishes were in the sink, newspapers littered every table. Old clothes were in piles on the floor. Quickly, he picked up a pair of socks, wrinkled his nose, and scooped the rest of his laundry up in his arms.

He had time to do a quick clean up, then pick up Wes and Claire.

Yep, he'd gotten his way. Now he just hoped his way had been the right one.

Chapter Six

"Isn't the fire great?"

"It's super. And warm." Claire forced herself to concentrate on the flames in front of her instead of where her mind kept turning to…the man sitting next to her on the thick sheepskin rug. But as she hugged her knees close to her chest, Claire had to admit that at the moment she couldn't care less about how much heat the fire was giving off.

All she really cared about was that Ty was sitting pretty darn close to her. And he smelled good, too.

Not that she was actively trying to uh, smell him.

Still, anyone would agree he was attractive, like most twenty-eight-year-old men. Fact was, Ty Slattery was the type of guy women checked out when they thought no one could see them doing it.

If she did her best to look at him completely objectively, Claire could probably name a bunch of reasons why Ty wasn't all that gorgeous, in a magazine-cover-model way. First off, he wasn't especially slim.

Weighing around two hundred pounds, he looked like a former football player who now didn't exercise as much as he used to. He also kept his hair cut short, really short, and his eyes were nothing special.

Just really, really blue. With short little jet black eyelashes that looked like they clung to each eyelid for dear life, just to frame those irises in the best possible way.

And his smile, it was striking but flawed. A couple of his teeth were not quite perfect. One of his incisors was kind of crooked, like he'd gotten it shifted during a fight or wrestling match and never cared too much about getting it fixed. And then there was his nose. It, too, looked like it had lost more than one round to an opponent.

A vainer man would have had it reset.

But maybe all those things encouraged Claire to look at him more often than not. Because he wasn't perfect, because his flaws were pronounced, she felt that hers maybe weren't so glaring.

Maybe.

"If you stare at those flames any longer, you're gonna get a sunburn or go cross-eyed," Ty teased.

Well, at least he thought she'd been focused on the fire! "I like looking at a roaring fire." *Oh, yeah, fireplaces are my thing.* Claire resisted rolling her eyes and hoped that he'd just forget she ever sounded so inane.

"Well, that's…good."

Yep, he thought she was ridiculous. Seeking to rectify things, she added, "Remember, I'm not around a fireplace all that often." *Oh, yeah, much better!*

Ty shifted. His movement pushed off half the blanket that had rested on his shoulders. "Thank God you decided to come sit by this one tonight. I'd have been worried about you two if you'd stayed at your place."

"We'd be pretty cold, that's for sure," Claire admitted. Even though the fire did warm things up, it had to be sixty degrees in the room…and would probably get worse. The last weather report indicated that the skies were clearing, so the temperatures would likely plunge into the single digits.

To their right, Wes was asleep in a thick sleeping bag. Curled next to him was Maisy. Claire wondered if the dog had joined the boy for the warmth or for Wes's total attention. All night Wes had either petted or played with the retriever. Ty had even commented that Maisy probably hadn't received so much attention in years.

Both Wes and the big dog had drifted off into a dead sleep after the three of them had finished playing their fifth game of Clue. Claire knew from experience that nothing was going to rouse her boy from his deep sleep except a natural disaster. So, they were effectively alone.

Leaving Claire to focus on Ty and everything she shouldn't be thinking.

Curving his hands around a knee, Ty looked at her steadily. "Ever care to tell me what you are around a lot?"

He'd lost her. "What do you mean?"

"If not fireplaces and cozy nights like this—what? You're so private. Is it your nature or are you just reluctant to be open around me?"

She paused to consider. "I'm not sure," she admitted. "Both, I guess. Plus, I'm not all that interesting."

His gaze softened in the flickering light. "Some might think otherwise."

"Not my son." Her heart beat a little faster, which was really embarrassing, because this had to be the tamest conversation Ty had probably ever had with a woman in the middle of the night. "Wes tells me I'm way too boring."

"Your boy has one person on his mind…Wes Grant. It's how all teenagers are. Weren't you that way? I know I was."

"It's been a long time since I thought about how I used to be."

He stretched out. His wool-covered feet moved a little closer to the flames, encouraging her eyes to trace just how well he filled out a pair of jeans. Just how different his arms were compared to hers, how at ease he was with his body. "How did you used to be, Claire?"

Her response came from the heart. "Silly."

A grin flashed. "Yeah? I can't imagine that. You seem so serious now."

"I've had to be. Things have happened…." Her voice drifted off. How much did she want to reveal? How much would he even want to hear? People didn't like sob stories. "Tell me about you. How serious are you?"

"Plenty serious when I have to be. Other times, not so much. And I'll tell you about me another time."

"Ty—"

"Come on. I asked first."

She still wasn't ready. "Ty…what is Ty short for?"

"Tyrus."

"I've never heard of such a name."

"I don't think my parents did, either," he said with a wry grin. "They foisted a heck of a name on me, Tyrus Abraham Slattery."

"It's got a nice ring to it."

"Not during roll call. I used to ask my dad why they

couldn't just have named me Tom." Leaning a little closer, he murmured, "Are you ever going to answer me?"

"I guess I have to now. I mean, if you can share your whole name, I can share a bit, too. I used to be Claire Amanda Rowan."

"Claire Amanda is pretty. Now you're Claire Amanda Grant?"

"Yep." Little by little, she fed him another bit of information, amazed at just how hard it was to give away any of her personal life. "I got married to Ray a few months after high school."

"Couldn't wait to get married?"

"No. I got pregnant with Wes." Thinking of that time, so long ago, when she'd pretended to everyone that she was in love. That she didn't care about never going to nursing school. That she didn't mind that Ray drank so much…it all brought back hurt. "It was a huge mistake."

"Ray?"

"Oh, yes, Ray. *He* was a huge mistake, never Wes." With a fond look her son's way, she added, "Wes is my rock."

"And then? After you got married and had Wes?"

Claire blanched. What could she say? No matter how good things had turned out, the simple truth was that she'd gotten into so much trouble that she'd been forced to let a stranger take care of Wes for a month. What kind of mother did that?

"Things went bad."

"How?"

"I'd rather not talk about it."

"Okay." After a moment, he blurted, "Did Ray hurt you?"

That almost made her smile. Patience was not one of Ty's virtues. As for her ex-husband—Ray had been difficult and volatile. A gambler and an alcoholic. He'd been unhappy and so had she. And he'd taken his anger out on her more than once. Those times were still too difficult to talk about. "Let's just say I know what it's like to be in a place where you wish you weren't."

After a moment, he nodded. "Enough said."

Thank the Lord! "Enough said."

Outside, the wind picked up, battering the windows with shards of ice. Little wisps of wind snaked through the old window wells, reminding them both that the worst storm in years wasn't over yet.

WHEN CLAIRE SHIVERED, Ty moved closer. "I'm sorry, I'd hoped things would be a little warmer in here."

"I'm fine."

Her face was pale, but Ty couldn't tell if it was from their earlier conversation and the many mixed-up feelings it brought back or whether it was from him. Was she worried about being alone with him?

He really hoped she wasn't. The last thing in the world he wanted her to worry about was whether or not she could trust him.

Because she could. Claire was one of the most decent people he'd ever met. There was no way he was going to do anything to make her uncomfortable.

He patted the floor, which was covered with wool blankets, down pillows and another two sleeping bags. "Do you think you'll be warm enough here?"

Claire pointed to her sock-covered feet. "I'll be fine."

She didn't look fine; she looked cold. Mentally, he walked through the Rubbermaid container in the back closet. In it, he had some outdoor gear for hunting—a few things left over from weekend trips with his dad during high school. "Hey, I've got a down parka that will be no trouble—"

"Stop, Ty," she said, gently placing a hand on his arm. To his surprise, the muscle jumped at her touch.

Ty stared at her hand. How could something so small affect him so much? What was it about Claire? How come he was so attracted to her?

Still holding onto his arm, she murmured, "You go get yourself that parka, I'm just fine."

He couldn't resist any longer. Running a hand down her arm, to where her fingers rested near his wrist, he caressed her soft skin. A flash of awareness flicked in her gaze, igniting him as much as if he'd just held her in his arms. "You sure?"

"Positive." She broke contact. Patting the comforter underneath them, she grinned. "This is kind of fun, actually. It's been a long time since I've had anyone to talk to after Wes goes to sleep."

"I know what you mean. It's almost like a campout."

"Almost." Her pupils had dilated. For the first time, no nervousness hinted in their depths. Instead, he saw very clearly the same thing he was feeling…heat.

That, of course, caused a spark of interest. Ty tamped it down. He had no intention on doing anything to spook her. He had a feeling a whole lot had taken place between her and her ex-husband. Taking care to keep his voice neutral, he said, "Sleeping on the ground like this reminds me of doing things with my dad. He and I used to go on camping trips when I was little."

"We camped, too. We had an old camper that fit all

three of us." She curved her fingers around the fluffy pink socks. Ty couldn't tell whether she was curving herself in from all the hurts or merely reminiscing. "Hmm. I hadn't thought of that in years."

"Where did y'all go camping? We went around Grand Lake."

"We never went too far. Just one of the old KIA sites in southern Ohio. But it didn't matter," Claire said, her voice wistful. "There was something about cooking dinner over a fire that was always so special."

"And s'mores."

"Oh, I loved s'mores."

"Ever have eggs cooked in biscuits? My dad was a fan of those."

"My mom made pancakes." She closed her eyes. "Lots and lots of pancakes." When she opened her eyes again, she shrugged. "Both of them are gone, now. That's hard to believe."

Ty wondered what had happened to them, but he didn't dare ask. Their past conversations had taught him to pick and choose his questions or he'd scare her half to death. He didn't want that. No, he wanted Claire to be comfortable around him.

And that was surprising in itself.

What was it about late nights and flickering fires that made a person want to divulge all their secrets? To dream about things best left forgotten…about things better left unsaid?

Ignoring his earlier vow, Ty said, "Is it just me or is it all men that you're not interested in?"

He didn't think she was going to answer. It would serve

him right if she didn't. That question had no place in their relationship, no place yet, anyway.

"Both," she finally said.

He was dying to ask her to clarify. Both, what? Both, forever?

As if she read his mind, she explained. "My marriage with Ray changed me. I'm afraid I'm not relationship material."

"Not right now?"

With a look of finality, she shook her head. "No, not right now. Not tomorrow, either. Probably not for a very long time."

He'd never met anyone who was so ready to give up on relationships. To give up on a future.

Well, besides himself.

Chapter Seven

Though he was afraid of where their conversation was taking them, he said, "Giving up on love at thirty-two? That's kind of harsh, don't you think?"

Ty watched the flames cast an orange-and-red glow across her features as she considered his question. He hoped she had taken him seriously. Was taking them seriously.

"Saying I'm not ready for a relationship and won't be for some time probably is harsh. But it doesn't change how things are. Sometimes what's harsh is what matters. The whole world can't be sunshine and daffodils."

"Maybe no one's asking for it to be. Maybe some people you know realize that sometimes the world's all about ice storms and power outages." *And sunshine and daffodils,* he mentally added.

Her eyes widened. "You sound like you know what I'm talking about. Do you?"

Ty shifted on the floor and finally moved to go sit with his back to the couch. "I might, more than you realize. I had a girlfriend in college…a serious one. Sharon. I thought we were going to marry."

"What happened?"

"Medical school and residency."

"Too much school?"

"Yeah. Way too much school and too many hours away from her." It had actually been the monster loans he'd taken out for medical school. But he wasn't in any hurry to talk about that with Claire.

He didn't really like talking about himself or Sharon, so Ty skimmed over that rocky situation as best he could. "Anyway, I know what it's like to lose someone I thought was going to be by my side for a lifetime."

"Ty, I'm sorry."

"Don't be." He spied pity in her eyes and he certainly didn't want that. "It all worked out for the best, anyway. I learned to count on the one person I could. Me."

"And you got through it."

He shrugged. "And I got through it."

Claire said softly, "You wouldn't believe it, but I'm jealous of that—jealous of being so self-sufficient. For a long time I wanted to depend only on myself but I wasn't able to. I didn't have the skills to."

The way she said it made Ty see that she was still embarrassed about her faults. Well, so was he. "Who did you depend on?"

After a pause, she said, "Strangers. Actually, I made friends with a gal named Tessa who had met Wes in a back alley."

This time he was the one who was struggling to keep the surprise out of his voice. "What?"

"We'd taken to collecting cans for gas and food money." For a second, she hid her face in her knees. "I can't believe I just told you that. When I hear myself talk about my past, I still can't believe I'm talking about me. When I was younger, I would have never imagined I would end up homeless." Slowly, she met his gaze. "It's still painful to admit."

Ty was still trying to get his arms around the fact that Claire and Wes had been foraging in dirty, dangerous Dumpsters. "Collecting cans?"

"We became pretty good at it."

"I can't believe you went through so much."

She shrugged. "We both work in a hospital. We both see people in tough situations all the time. What happened to me is sad but not unique."

"How long were you homeless?"

"Four awful, never-ending months." Patting the comforter underneath her once again, like she was checking to see that it was still there, she grimaced. "Now those days seem like a dream. It felt like one while we were going through it, as a matter of fact. All I did was try to get through each hour, each day."

"That was probably the best way to cope."

"Coping?" She shook her head, not meeting his eyes. "Coping means you can take care of yourself. That you take what you get and make the best of things. That wasn't what I did. Instead, I think I fostered a healthy case of denial. And then, well, I got sick. Really sick."

"What happened?"

"I got pneumonia. A bad case." As if she was afraid of lying, Claire spit out a few more morsels of information. "I was malnourished. It was tough on Wes." She rolled her eyes. "That's an understatement. No child should have to see a parent in the condition I was in."

Ty could only compare her story with his mother's. When things got bad at his house, his mom took off. She'd left him with a dad who didn't have any more soft feelings in him—who'd had no idea about what to do with a boy except push him into sports.

At the time, Ty had thought it was because his dad hadn't wanted him around. Now, maybe, he thought it was because he knew Ty was going to need to develop the skills necessary to succeed in life.

Though he had no kids, Ty was learning that all someone could do was stick around and do the best that he or she could. And Claire had.

With that in mind, he murmured, "Things were tough on you, too. Claire, you're lucky you didn't die."

"Anyway, one night, Wes found Tessa, who managed a fancy boutique and asked for help. She saw me, called a cop friend of hers and, next thing anyone knew, I was being admitted in the hospital and Tessa was volunteering to take care of my son."

"I can't imagine how strong you must have been," he commented, moving off the couch and back next to her.

"I wasn't strong, Ty. In fact, I was just the opposite. I messed everything up. I was running from bill collectors and too ignorant of social services to even know who to ask for help. I was scared to death that someone would see what a horrible job I was doing with Wes and take him away. I put my needs and worries way before my son's and paid the price, dearly."

"But it all worked out. Nobody did take him away, did they?"

"No," she murmured. "Nobody did."

Another burst of wind shot through the gaps around the windows. By mutual consent, they moved closer to the fire. With each movement, their bodies brushed closer. Ty could smell her shampoo.

Claire shivered, then kept talking. "I tell Tessa that she is surely my guardian angel, she was so kind. Wes lived with Tessa for almost a month. I stayed in the hospital for two weeks, then started working there."

"You're amazing," he murmured.

"Oh, stop. If I were 'amazing,' I wouldn't have gotten in that situation in the first place."

Unable to stop himself, Ty reached out and touched her. He brushed the back of two fingers against her cheek. "I think Ray caused the trouble, not you."

"Okay then, if I were amazing, I wouldn't have married the wrong man for all the wrong reasons." She looked away and his hand fell to his side. "All that experience does is remind me that I can't give up or give in ever again. I need to take care of myself and be strong. Save. Plan for the future. Never be in debt again. And, most importantly, never depend on a man again." As if she realized that she was on a soapbox, she blushed. "Sorry. I didn't mean to sound so dramatic."

"You didn't," he replied. Then, before he could second guess himself or ask why he wanted to kiss her so badly… he just did.

Her lips were soft—that wasn't a surprise. What was stunning was the way in which Claire leaned toward him, turning so that she fit more securely in his embrace. He kissed her again, traced her lips with his tongue, was just about to delve a little deeper when Maisy groaned and Wes coughed in response.

Claire jumped back with a start. "Oh!"

Ty knew he should apologize. For what, he wasn't sure—the whole thing had seemed pretty mutual. But Claire did look confused and worried. "Sorry—I guess my mind left me for a second," he said.

"Mine, too." Then, to his pleasure, a wry smile appeared. "But—I'm not sorry we kissed."

Hunger rushed through him; to hide it he made a show of glancing at his watch. "Gosh, it's almost midnight. Maybe we should get some sleep?"

She crawled into her sleeping bag. "Sleep sounds… good." After a moment of silence—a strange, too-still moment of silence—she said, "I'll see you in the morning, Ty."

Yes, she would.

In the glow of firelight, Ty turned away from Claire and rolled into his own homemade cocoon. He punched at his pillows a couple of times, then lay back and thought about the woman sleeping nearby.

Claire had gotten it all wrong. He didn't want to save her. He wanted to get to know her. He just plain wanted her.

And he wanted her to want him.

Chapter Eight

"But if I say something to her, she's going to tell everyone else and then I'll really be in trouble," Wes said, in that tone of voice that said everything was both right and wrong, all at the same time.

It took a few moments for Claire to realize where she was. Living room floor of Ty Slattery's living room. Power outage.

"You think?" Ty said. His voice sounded gravelly, like he was a smoker, though Claire knew for sure that he wasn't. So, that voice had to be the product of a night spent tossing and turning on a hard wooden floor.

How come she'd slept so well?

"I know!" Wes proclaimed. "If I say anything it's going to be death."

Claire knew what she should do. She should sit up and announce that she was awake. But things had been so strange between her and Wes lately that she guiltily appreciated the new insight into his mind. Mind made up, she settled in and eavesdropped some more.

With her eyes closed, her other senses were on overdrive. They were cooking hot dogs over the flame of the fire and whispering pretty loud. Hot dogs in the morning… ugh!

But maybe that was another guy thing she'd never figured out.

"Maybe you shouldn't say anything yet, then," Ty said reasonably. "Sometimes women like a little mystery."

Mystery? What mystery? And why would Ty encourage Wes not to tell her about things? That sure didn't seem right. Claire just about started to say something when Wes spoke again.

"But if I don't say a word, then Leesa won't know I like her and I do."

Claire's mouth went dry. This was about a girl? Leesa? She didn't know Wes liked girls. She didn't know he thought about them one way or another!

"That's a tough one. Good thing it's Sunday so we can think about it for a while. I've learned it's best not to push things with girls, they get freaked out."

"Yeah. Chris Callahan said he was going to pass Leesa a note in gym on Monday. But here's the thing, Ty. I don't know what I'm supposed to write. What if I say something stupid and then Leesa goes and shows it to all her girl-friends? That would suck."

"I don't think I'm going to be able to help you with the whole note thing. Last time I wrote a note to a girl, it didn't work out so well."

Who was Ty talking about? Sharon?

CLANK!

"Oh, would you look at that, I dropped a skewer." As Ty bent down to get it, he caught a glance at Claire's suddenly opened eyes. "Sorry we woke you." Very deliberately, he gave a little wink.

"Oh, no problem." Claire made a production out of stretching.

After wiping her eyes, she groaned as she struggled to sit up. Even with the extra padding underneath her, she knew she was going to be sore from sleeping on the hard ground.

"So, what are you two men cooking and eating? Hot dogs?" She struggled to look surprised and impressed at the same time. "Right over the fire?"

Ty shrugged. "It was that or s'mores. These seemed the better choice."

"Thanks for that."

Wes grinned as he wiped the corner of his mouth with his hand, then rubbed his hand on the leg of his sweats. "Ty said hot dogs can be eaten at any time of day."

She shared a look with Ty. "Even for breakfast?"

"Especially for breakfast." Twirling a dog around a bit, he added, "You want one?"

"No, thanks. But if you could make some coffee in that fire, I'd be eternally grateful."

He pointed to an old fashioned looking kettle hanging from the end of a pair of fireplace tongs. "How does hot water and instant coffee sound?"

"Like heaven."

Struggling to her feet, she said, "Mind if I go get freshened up?"

"Freshen what, Mom?"

Ty cut him off neatly. "Down the hall. Fourth door on the left." He handed her a flashlight. "There's a bit of natural light coming through the beveled glass, but take this in case you need a bit more."

Claire picked up her makeup bag and scurried in, thankful for the privacy and the flashlight. In no time, she'd brushed her teeth, pulled back her hair, added a bit of mascara and a swipe of colored lip balm.

When she returned, Ty handed her a cup of coffee. "Do you want a little cream? With the cold air in here, the fridge hasn't had a chance to get warm yet."

"Thanks. I'll get it." She took the mug and walked toward the kitchen to exploit the chance she had to look around. It was definitely decorated in Man 101.

But, it was also the kitchen of a man who was completely self-sufficient. A couple of cookbooks rested in a bookshelf…*Betty Crocker. Better Homes and Gardens. Bobby Flay.* Two of the cupboards had glass inserts, so she could see that he had whole sets of stoneware in them. Some kind of sturdy, thick, gray and blue pieces that matched the mug in her hand.

There were no knickknacks around or other homey touches like on her counters. But there were three large mason jars filled with spices and such. Interesting.

The fridge was still cold. A carton of cream kept company with a half-gallon of milk, a six pack of beer, a couple of cans of Coke and more condiments than she'd ever seen in her life.

"I like to grill," he said over her shoulder.

"Sorry. I didn't mean to stand here, looking like I'm taking stock."

"Don't apologize. I'd have done the same thing if I was in front of your fridge. It's interesting to see how other people live."

Hastily, she poured a healthy dose of cream in her coffee and closed the refrigerator. When she sipped, she couldn't help but be surprised. "This is good."

Ty grinned. "You look shocked."

"I just never knew Folgers could taste so good."

"It's not Folgers. It's from a mail-order place." He shrugged. "I've learned over the years not to count on brewed coffee. Between emergencies at the hospital and my years in med school, I discovered that a good packet of instant can make the difference between lasting another four hours or another forty-five minutes."

"And power outages," she said.

"Yep. Wes and I were about to turn on the battery radio. Want to listen?"

"Sure."

"Mom, sure you don't want a hot dog?"

"I'm positive. This will do me."

Claire followed Ty back to the living room and pulled up a chair that they'd pushed back the night before to make way for all their bedding. It was cold, probably mid-fifties in the house. Wes was dressed in sweats and cozy in his down sleeping bag. Now that she wasn't stewing on his love life, she noticed how young he still looked—his eyes a little puffy, his freckled cheeks flushed. Hair going all which way.

She sipped her coffee, welcoming the liquid heat that slid downward.

A voice came on, announcing storm statistics and power outages. The three of them listened as the announcer said that most of southern Ohio was without power, more sleet and snow was expected within hours and emergency crews were going to be concentrating on shelters, nursing homes and hospitals first. Residential areas would follow.

"We're going to be in the dark for a while, I'm afraid," Ty said.

"Cool!" Wes exclaimed, his face a picture of happiness.

He went over to pet Maisy. Claire watched as the retriever shifted to allow him to pet her side and chest.

"I'm sorry you're stuck with us," she told Ty when Wes was out of earshot. "If I would have known that we were going to be here so long I would never have agreed to come over."

"Why? So you could sit in your place and be cold?"

"But it's an imposition. Isn't it?"

Thinking of their kiss last night, he did his best to play it cool and said, "Not at all."

"You sure?"

"Positive. If you weren't here, I'd be doing the same thing. Me and Miss Maisy would be sitting in the dark drinking instant coffee and listening to the weather report." He smiled to soften his matter-of-fact tone. "Trust me, this is better."

It might have been his imagination, but Ty felt there was an underlying tension between them. He couldn't put his finger on it. Didn't want to. But there was something there that felt different. Had their kiss brought that on? Or their conversation? He decided to tread very carefully in order not to scare her away.

"Mom, what are we going to do?"

"Sit and wait."

"How about cards?" Ty asked, thinking that was something they could all do together. "Do you all play hearts?"

"I haven't played hearts in ages," Claire said.

Ty noticed Wes looked mildly intrigued. "Want to play? I have to warn you, that I play to win. No special treatment for women and children."

"What do you get if you win?"

"Wes!"

Ty chuckled. He didn't know a lot about being around women and babies, but he remembered being a cocky teen. "I would say that the satisfaction of winning should be enough."

Wes directed a glare at his mom. "That's what she says. Always."

"How about we play for…pennies?" Ty grabbed an old water jug, half-full with loose change.

"All this change is cool," Wes said, eyeing the assortment of coins with such concentration that Ty was pretty sure he could see the wheels turning in his brain as he tried to calculate just how much money there was.

After fortifying them both with mugs of coffee and giving Wes some instant hot chocolate, they were in business. In no time at all, they'd relocated to the kitchen table and after a few trial runs, they were off and running.

One hour turned to two, then three. And just as Wes was yawning and Ty was wondering how to entertain the two of them next, the power clicked on. With a whoosh, heat began to blow from the vents. Two lights in the kitchen blinked, then burned brightly.

"Heat!" Wes stood up and put his hand over one of the vents. Maisy walked next to him and nudged the grate with her nose.

"Well, I guess our little vacation here is over." Claire neatly collected the cards and slid them back into the case.

"I can't thank you enough for your hospitality. When you have time to take us home, we'll get out of your hair."

Wes grunted. "Right now?"

Ty felt like a brother-in-arms with Wes, because he couldn't have put his feelings into better words. "Maybe you should think about hanging out here a while longer? You know how the electric lines are…a clump of snow could fall on one and we'd be in the dark again."

She pasted a wide, fake smile on. So fake that Ty wasn't sure if she was hiding relief or disappointment that they were going back home. "We'll take our chances. We've imposed on you long enough."

He was just about to let her have her way when his cell phone beeped and vibrated on the kitchen counter. "I've got to take this," he murmured, seeing it was the hospital. "Slattery."

"Ty, any chance you can come in?" the chief resident asked, sounding harried and stressed. "We've got five victims from a car accident and a full waiting room. We need everyone who's available ASAP."

"Give me fifteen minutes." Turning to Claire, he said, "I've got to go into work. Things are really busy."

"Oh. All right. Wes, run and get your things together. We'll be ready in a minute."

He knew he couldn't do it. He couldn't end their time together like that. He couldn't send her off with little more than a brief goodbye and a "see you later." For reasons he didn't care to examine, Ty wanted to know that while he was at the hospital, she and Wes were okay. "Would you mind staying here instead of having me run you home?"

"What?"

"By the time I change clothes and heat up the car, I'm barely going to have time to make it there—and there's no telling what the roads are like."

"But—"

He neatly cut her off. "If I had to drop you off, I'd feel like I had to go in and make sure everything was okay. I don't have the time."

Fire entered her gaze. "I would never ask you to check on me."

"I can't just leave you on the doorstep."

"I've been living on my own for quite a while. I don't need you to take care of me," Claire said, her face flushing.

Ty knew how to give orders that sounded like favors. When he'd been made captain of the varsity team, the coach had taught him how to lead. That skill had also come in handy in the OR. "Wes, would you help your mom take care of the place and walk Maisy while I'm gone?"

Wes's head popped up. "Sure."

"What would you like me to do?"

Ty knew he heard a sarcastic edge, but he glibly ignored it. "Could you make some soup or something? I've got beef and chicken in the freezer and some canned vegetables somewhere."

"Well, sure, but—"

"It's going to be nuts up there. I'd really appreciate it if I knew there was something to eat when I got back later. That is, if you don't mind."

"I don't mind." Her eyes narrowed on him for a second, then as if she'd finally decided she wasn't going to question him, she shrugged. "I'll be happy to make some soup. My pleasure."

"Great. Wes, come with me. We can talk while I throw on some clothes and shave." When the boy followed him, Ty said, "I know your mom's uncomfortable with this, but y'all will help me out by staying here. Are you okay with that?"

"Can I watch your TV?"

"Yep."

"I'm good."

"If you get bored, start rolling some of those coins for me, would you? I'd love to know how much is in there."

"You don't mind me touching your money?"

"I trust you."

Wes stood a little straighter. "Okay."

They talked for a few more minutes while Ty ran the water until it got warm, heated up a washcloth, then quickly shaved and washed his face. Next, he pulled out a pair of khakis and a button-down, his usual attire, and just to be on the safe side he packed a spare.

Wes noticed. "Why are you packing clothes?"

Ty decided not to make a big deal about it. "Two reasons. One, I may be at the hospital longer than I think. Two, you never know what's going to get on your clothes."

"Eww."

After grabbing a knit cap and a pair of gloves, he picked up his tote and headed to the door. "Claire, thanks."

She merely nodded. "Would you mind if I asked you to give me a call in a couple of hours? I'll, uh, want to know that you're okay."

"Mom, he's not a kid."

"I know." She wrung her hands. "It's silly, but if you don't mind—"

"I don't mind. I was planning on it. I'm glad you care."

As HE DROVE the treacherous roads to Lane's End Memorial, Ty saw at least five cars abandoned or victims of fender benders. If that was any indication, he was going to be really busy.

But for the first time in memory, he actually was going to have someone who noticed.

Ty didn't dare try to analyze why he appreciated that so much.

Chapter Nine

Claire stood at the window for a good long time after she and Wes watched Ty back out in his Jeep, then slowly make his way down the snowy, icy road. In the distance, she heard snow plows and was grateful that he'd be on the main streets soon. She knew that they'd have the streets around the hospital plowed and salted before anyone got to residential side streets.

Her concern for Ty caught her by surprise. Though if she were honest with herself, the last twenty-four hours had felt off-kilter.

Things weren't happening like they usually did. She wasn't wishing things were better or different or nursing a pain in her stomach the size of a grapefruit. No, she was comfortable. Almost.

"What do you think, sport?"

Wes was sitting on the leather couch, managing to look comfortable and awkward at the same time. "It's weird, being here."

"I know. But I couldn't very well make him to take us home—not when he was needed at the hospital."

"I don't mind being here. It's a lot nicer than our place. And Ty's cool." Wes paused. "You think he likes you?"

He had sure acted like it last night. "Maybe," she hedged, fighting the impulse to tell Wes that her love life wasn't any of his business. But it kind of was. Any relationship she had would affect him as much as her.

"You know."

"All right, then." Claire took a breath, knowing what she wanted to say. She wanted to say no. But men didn't offer dinner and sleepovers to mere acquaintances. Or kiss charity cases. There was definitely something between them. "I think he might," she said hesitantly. "Does that bother you?"

Wes didn't answer right away, which was telling, because it meant that he was taking things seriously. Finally, he said, "I thought it would but it doesn't. Well, not that much."

"Because of his house?" She joked.

"No. Because being here feels…normal."

Claire didn't need him to explain what that meant. Being with Ty did feel normal.

"How about you go take a shower, then I'll start laundry?" Since she was going to be all domestic, she might as well get a lot done. She had no desire to pass the day on the couch.

"I don't need to shower."

"Yeah, you do. You slept all night next to the dog on the floor."

Wes shrugged and walked down the hall. Maisy followed. When the door shut, the old retriever lay down with a sigh next to the closed door, just waiting for Wes to come back out.

The sight brought a lump to Claire's throat. Wes had always wanted a dog and she'd always wanted stability for him. Of course now wasn't the time, she worked full time, then ran Wes around to wrestling practices and tournaments. But seeing her son and Maisy reminded Claire that some things were still possible. Even dreams and things she had imagined but thought could never be.

When she heard the shower start, Claire went into the kitchen and washed dishes from the picnic that morning, then took inventory of Ty's supplies. He wasn't kidding… despite the preponderance of Hungry-Man dinners, he had a fully stocked freezer and pantry. Obviously the man was a regular Boy Scout—always prepared for everything.

As soon as she spied barley, she decided to make a thick beef stew.

Wes came out, clothes in hand. She grabbed sheets, Wes's clothes, then did what she'd been dreading. She ventured into Ty's bedroom to find his laundry basket. From the dark tan sheets to the books and papers on his dresser to the pile of clothes thrown on a chair, it all screamed Ty.

That old familiar lump in her stomach came roaring back, but this time it had nothing to do with remembered dreams and everything to do with an attraction that she hadn't counted on and had certainly never asked for.

Oh, but his room smelled good. It beckoned her inside, practically calling her name and asking her to take a peek.

When she heard the TV click back on, Claire felt confident that she had a little bit of privacy. Deciding to take advantage of it, she wandered over to his dresser and peeked at the cologne. Eddie Bauer.

Claire smiled. It was nothing too fancy but so perfect

for Ty: outdoorsy, masculine, steady. Not too showy but well made.

That thought made her sit down on his bed. It practically bounced back at her. It was one of those fancy Temper-pedic mattresses that she and Wes had looked at in a specialty store in the mall. It was all about helping bad backs and ensuring a good night's rest. Claire wondered if it actually worked.

Five—no, six—pillows lay at the top. Six pillows for one man? If he hadn't told her differently, she would have imagined that he had a girlfriend who spent the night regularly.

Wes changed the channels and, fearing she was about to be discovered, Claire picked up her pace. Quickly, she ran to the bathroom. A black marble countertop ran the length of one wall. Above it rested a series of large silver-framed mirrors. An antique looking tub sat on the other side. Above it was a chrome oval with a sheer white shower curtain. Tan and ivory towels lay everywhere…so much so that Claire couldn't tell which towels were dirty and which were clean. She played it safe and picked them all up to wash.

To stop herself from inspecting his things even more, Claire made a beeline for his clothes hamper—a canvas and chrome contraption—snagged an armful of laundry and scurried out.

Do not even think about looking at his clothes, she warned herself rigidly. You do that, you'll know you've got serious problems. If Wes sees you doing such a thing, he'll know you've gone off the deep end!

With that in mind, she hastily checked each item to

make sure she wasn't tossing a fancy shirt only made to dry clean in the washer, then clicked on the machine.

Water started pouring out just as Wes and Maisy surfaced again. "Hey!"

Claire forced herself to act naturally, as if she wasn't still thinking about men's boxers. "Hey. You okay?"

"Yep. Guess what?" He smiled, reaching down to pet Maisy. "When I came out of the shower, Maisy was right there waiting for me."

"I saw that. The moment you went inside, she lay right down."

Maisy's tail started to thump and she let out a little contented rumble, leading Wes to plop down on the ground beside her and pet her some more. The golden retriever squirmed in ecstasy and crawled closer. In no time she laid her muzzle on Wes's thigh. As Wes scratched the retriever's ears, his voice turned wistful. "I always wanted a dog."

"I know. Something tells me Maisy's always wanted a boy, too."

"We could get our own."

She knew that wheedling tone. And before they could replay conversations that had already been spoken time and again, she pointed to the fridge. "You hungry?"

"Not yet. Do you think it would be okay if I watched one of Ty's DVDs while I rolled coins?"

"I think it would be just fine. Don't forget to count the coins carefully before you put them in the papers."

His shoulders stiffened. "I will."

"Oh. Well, let me show you how to get started."

"I've rolled coins before, Mom," he said impatiently.

"We did it once in school, for the penny war. Don't you remember?"

"Now I do." The mention of the penny war reminded her of when that had happened. They'd been homeless. They'd had no pennies to donate….

Those days were long gone. Hopefully, they'd stay that way, as long as she didn't do anything stupid, like forget what was important: security.

But Wes didn't need to be reminded of that. "Since you don't need any help from me, I'm going to make some stew. You go get busy."

After a curious look at her abrupt dismissal, Wes led Maisy over to the TV, played with the remote for a while, then ended up watching an old Indiana Jones movie while counting the coins.

Claire found herself defrosting steak in the micro-wave—making dinner for her son and a man who had opened up his house, his life to her.

And it was taking everything she had to remind herself that what was happening was not real.

It couldn't be.

SEVEN HOURS from the time he'd gotten out of the house, Ty climbed into his vehicle. As the vehicle warmed up, he called home. After two rings, Claire hesitantly answered. "Dr. Slattery's home."

That made him smile. "Hey, Claire. You sound awfully professional, answering my phone like that."

"Oh, stop. I thought it was you, but I wasn't positive, so I thought I'd better play it safe. How are you? How were things at the hospital?"

"They were about what you'd expect."

"Hmm. Nervous people. A few broken bones from slips on the ice. One or two car accidents?"

He heard the smile in her voice and for what seemed like the first time since the morning, he smiled, too. "You got it."

"Any problems?"

"Nothing I couldn't handle." For a moment, as the Jeep warmed and the cool air turned into warm air, he reflected on just how nice it was to speak with somebody who actually knew what was going on in the hospital. Things had gotten hairy, but her acknowledgment of his job felt like a warm balm.

The fact that he had wanted that—had needed that—caught him off guard.

"So, are you okay?" she asked.

"I'm good. Tell me about you."

"Well…Wes and I have been busy counting coins and putting things in order." Her voice sounded cheery and content. It made him smile in anticipation. "I've got stew all ready for you. It smells heavenly, if I do say so myself."

"I can't wait to have some. Do you need anything?"

"Just you."

There went his body.

And uncomfortable silence flared on the line. Just when Ty was trying to think of something to say to set them both at ease, Claire stuttered on her end of the line. "Scratch that. Gosh, I didn't mean it how it sounded. I mean, we're just waiting for you. To come home. I mean, to come back to *your* house."

He knew what she meant. But he also knew how she felt. It had been a long time since he'd had a reason to hurry home. Since he'd had the feelings of anxiousness. It felt good. Welcome.

"I'm leaving now. See you soon." Ty clicked off before either of them said anything else they'd regret.

Chapter Ten

Claire had never been more aware of a man than she was of Ty Slattery. From the moment he'd arrived, showered and sat across from her at his kitchen table, there'd been an almost otherworldly quality about how she felt around him. Every sense was on alert…she noticed each look, each sip of beer, each time his lips curved into a smile.

Everything about him struck her as unique and interesting and, time and again, Claire found herself mesmerized by all things Ty.

After a hearty dinner of her homemade stew, Wes showed off just how many coins he'd rolled. There were easily thirty neatly rolled stacks of quarters, dimes, nickels and pennies in a basket on the kitchen counter, with plenty more in the jar waiting their turn.

Then Claire watched how well Ty's magic worked on Wes. He told Wes that when they were all rolled, the two of them would decide together what to spend the money on. Her boy glowed from the attention. Her gushing and praise was faint, indeed, compared to Ty's reaction.

Afterward, Ty asked Wes to help him shovel the

driveway. To Claire's surprise, Wes agreed without complaint. In fact, he kind of swaggered outside, like he was off to do "man's work." Now, how funny was that? Wes usually made a fuss when she asked him to make his bed.

An hour later, both came in with bright pink cheeks and light sweats. She served them both hot chocolate with marshmallows, then sent Wes to the shower.

And now, Ty poured them each a tumbler full of Bailey's on ice and sat beside her on his worn leather couch. Just like they had a relationship.

After being around him and in his place all day, Claire knew they did.

"I'm going to bed," Wes called out.

"Good night," Claire said. She turned just in time to catch a glimpse of her son, wrapped in an extra large chocolate-colored bath sheet, padding down into the guest room.

Ty raised an eyebrow. "I would have never guessed he'd go to bed so willingly."

For the first time in hours, Claire felt she had the advantage. "Hmm. It must be something to do with the queen-size bed, down comforter, DVD player and flat-screen TV in that bedroom." Thinking of Wes's very normal-looking twin bed, old chest of drawers and bookshelf of adventure novels, she added, "It's a far cry from his room at home."

"It's a far cry from my usual way of life, too. Dr. Michaels fixed this place up really nice. I can't believe I'm lucky enough to live here."

"You deserve it. This place suits you, Ty."

"Thanks. Well, anyway, I'm glad Wes is going to put that TV to good use. He worked hard outside."

Like any mother would, she beamed. "He's a hard

worker. He always has been." She sipped from her iced drink, letting the thick liquor slide down her throat and pool in her stomach, warming it.

Her stomach clenched and she knew it had nothing to do with the liquor and everything to do with the company. Yet again, she was supremely aware of their bodies next to each other and her attraction to him. To her surprise, her current attraction wasn't based on their past or even their present—at the moment it was all pheromones.

She looked for something to say. "Thanks for letting us sleep here tonight. Again."

"I should be the one thanking you. Claire, coming home to you both, with a warm dinner prepared...I can't tell you how nice it was. I haven't looked forward to a night like tonight in a long time." He paused to sip from his own drink. "It was such a great surprise to discover that you did all my laundry, too. You didn't have to, you know."

"I didn't mind." Though now that she knew he favored brightly colored boxers, she knew she'd never look at him the same.

Oh, who was she kidding? She hadn't ever been able to look at him the same way she looked at other men. There was something about Ty that drew her to him. She'd caught herself peeking to catch a glimpse of him at the hospital or wrestling meets more than a time or two.

In front of them, the fire crackled to life as a log split in two. A few sparks hit the black mesh screen, lighting like fireflies, then fading to black in the space of a blink.

But the air between them felt just as alive and fiery.

Ty shifted, bringing his body closer. Now, his arm rested

on the back of the couch. If they'd been younger, she would have guessed that he was making a move on her on purpose. But grown men didn't do things like that, did they?

Surely, someone of Ty's experience would have more practiced, suave moves…right? He'd already admitted he'd been serious with Sharon. Claire would be shocked if he hadn't had a lot of experience dating. A man with looks like his didn't live like a monk.

"Want to watch television?"

She couldn't care less about what was on television, but it would give her something else to focus on. Anything but Ty's arm almost over her shoulders. "Sure."

He clicked on different stations, finally settling on an old episode of *CSI*. As the detectives on the screen uncovered a particularly gruesome-looking corpse, Ty lowered his arm, curving his hand around her shoulder. His fingers played with the ends of her hair. "Guess this isn't the best show to watch for romance, huh?"

Romance? "It depends if you're wanting to be romantic or not." She did her best to sound easygoing and relaxed. Like she sat on couches with men wrapping their arms around her shoulders all the time. But it was so far from the truth it was laughable.

On the screen, two detectives were uncovering another body, this one dead from multiple stab wounds. Blood was everywhere.

All Claire could think about was how attune she was to Ty's body. To how good it felt to be next to him. How ready she was to kiss him. She was so ready for another kiss.

She was so ready for a lot of things.

"I haven't had sex since Ray," she blurted.

As her words filled the air, they sounded stark and pathetic. Desperate. Stalker-like. *Oh…damn!*

Ty glanced at her quickly. Down went his arm.

Damn again! Claire felt her cheeks heat. Yep, now she sounded desperate *and* needy.

Hastily she said, "I'm going to go check on Wes." Padding down the hall barefoot, she peeked in his room. His television was tuned to CSI, too. But he was sound asleep.

She turned off the TV and lights, then gathered her courage to join Ty again. Because, really, what was the worst that could happen?

He'd think she was now not only sleeping at his home, but wanting to sleep with him.

Ty looked up as she came back in. "How's Wes?"

"Asleep." She felt his gaze skim over her as she sat down next to him again. "I think all that shoveling and the lack of sleep last night has finally taken its toll."

"Has the day taken its toll on you, too?"

"Oh, I don't know." But that was a lie. Everything that had gone on in the last forty-eight hours had taken its toll. She was thinking about things that she'd carefully suppressed for ten years. Thinking about making love with Ty. Imagining what it would be like to be in his arms. To kiss him. To feel his hands along her body, caressing her.

The fire crackled. She jumped.

She sipped her drink for comfort. Of course, that just shot another surge right through her.

Very gently, he unwrapped her fingers from around the glass and linked his fingers through hers. His hands felt large and capable.

"So…how long has it been? Since Ray?"

This was her fault. If she'd never said a word about her lack of love life, she wouldn't be having to explain herself. She deserved every bit of her discomfort.

She did.

"Almost four years." As she said the words, she knew in her heart that it had been far longer. They hadn't been intimate at all their last year of marriage. Ray'd been drinking and gone so much.

And because Ty's eyes, so gentle and understanding— or maybe it was the Bailey's—she amended her words. "More like five. Maybe six. It's, ah, been a while."

Though she didn't know what to expect…because she'd never had the strength to admit so much to anyone, she prepared herself for a joke. A question. It was only natural for him to be curious about her past.

But he didn't do any of that. "Six years is a long time."

It had been. Pretty much an eternity. Looking at their joined fingers, Ty said, "It's been a while for me, too."

"Not six years, I hope."

He almost smiled. "No, not six years, thank God." Ty paused, moved a little closer. Very tenderly, he brushed hair off her shoulder and traced the exposed spot of skin in between her neck and the neckline of her sweater with one finger. She shuddered, feeling the repercussions of that touch as strongly as if he'd touched her in far more intimate places.

He noticed. Two fingers ran along the nape of her neck, along the blood vessels carrying blood to her heart. Her pulse jumped.

But nothing felt as jarring as his next words.

"Claire, I haven't wanted to make love with anyone in a long time."

"I understand." Did she? All she could think about was Ty's fingers on her bare skin. Think about his lips replacing them. About removing her sweater and doing the stuff that dreams were made of. Well, her dreams of long ago.

"I know you do," Ty said quietly. Like they were discussing the weather. Or work schedules. Or beef stew. "That's why I'm hoping you'll know what I mean when I say that I haven't wanted to be with anyone for a long time. I haven't wanted to make love with any woman…until you."

Well, there it was. A punch to the heart. She felt as exposed and wanted as if she were a movie star in a glossy men's magazine.

Claire knew she could do one of two things. She could pretend she didn't know what he meant. Didn't know what he was asking. Or she could follow his lead.

What was funny was that for the first time, it felt like everything was in her court. Like she was in charge. Instinctively, Claire knew that if she told Ty that she wasn't ready, that he wasn't the one or that this wasn't the place, he'd accept it without a fight.

But being close to him sounded so good. And after what seemed like a lifetime of doing things because she had to do them…or doing things because she had no choice, because they were good for her, good for Wes, or good for her future, all she wanted at that very moment was to feel. She wanted to feel wanted and special because she was still a person—a woman. Not homeless or sick or needy but attractive and pretty and important.

And given that she knew exactly what it felt like not to feel that way, she knew there was no choice. None worth thinking about, anyway. "I feel the same way."

Blue eyes blinked. "You sure?"

"I've never been more sure."

Ty stood up and held out a hand. She took it and followed him to the bedroom. He closed it behind them. Locked it.

And took her in his arms. Then Claire finally kissed him again.

Ty was taller than she was. A good six inches. But when he lowered his head and she rose up on her tiptoes, their differences felt right.

One kiss turned to several, each one more passionate and hot than the next. His mouth opened. Hers did, too. Tongues and teeth and lips met and darted against each other.

No, neither had done much in a very long time. But they hadn't forgotten how to make love. And Claire, now that she'd made her decision, couldn't wait to experience everything all over again. Even if it was just for one night.

Ty moaned as his hands brushed down her back, under her sweater. Curved along her bare skin. Fingers searched the indent of her spine, traced the outline of her rib cage.

They had on way too many clothes.

Claire pulled off her sweater. Ty did the same with his shirt. Her bra went next. Followed by two pairs of jeans and those boxers.

Last went a pair of very serviceable pink cotton panties.

The room was dim. Outside, the air was silent; every sound and look felt magnified.

"Claire," Ty murmured, stepping closer, holding her against him. Thigh to thigh. Skin to skin. Her breasts flattened against his smooth chest.

They moved to his bed. Kisses deepened, became more heated. Ty's mouth roamed. She did her best to keep up.

Smiles took the place of long-ago disappointments. Warm gazes of appreciation replaced feelings of insecurity. And Ty's loving words right before he entered her made Claire feel wanted and perfect.

And that feeling was worth any price. Worth any past mistakes.

Everything would have been perfect if one little troubling thought hadn't just reared its tiny head.

She hadn't used any birth control. Neither had Ty.

And that was how Wes had come to be.

Chapter Eleven

"Wes—" Claire said.

"Is fine." Ty covered her mouth with his, preventing her from saying anything more.

"No, I mean—" Her eyes widened as he nipped along her jaw, slid his hand down her body.

"Hush, Claire." After the night they'd had, he still wanted her, still felt like he couldn't get enough of her. When she gasped, he took the opportunity to deepen the kiss.

She'd been passionate. Sweet and tempting, giving and unique. Making love with Claire hadn't been the stuff of adolescent dreams. No, it was the kind of thing a grown man looked forward to. And he could definitely imagine looking forward to being in her arms every night.

"Wes is asleep, remember?" Ty asked, all the while taking care to not miss an inch of blessed, perfect skin between her neck and her breasts.

Propping herself on her elbows, Claire shook her head. "That's not what I'm talking about."

Ty forced himself to sit back. To look at her face. "What's wrong? Are you okay? Was I too rough?" He hadn't remembered being rough, though. He'd loved her tenderly, slowly, savoring the gift she'd given him.

She shook her head, her eyes warming unmistakably. "You weren't rough at all. Actually, I…I didn't know a man could be so gentle."

Her words shamed him. He'd forgotten how she'd flinched when he'd first touched her in the parking lot. He hated the thought of another man abusing her. "I'm sorry you didn't know gentleness before."

Confusion, replaced by fear, replaced by happiness entered her eyes. "It doesn't matter now. Now I know the difference."

He kissed her eyelids, his touch feather-soft.

To his surprise, heat filled her eyes when she opened them again. "I'm not delicate, Ty. I promise I'm not."

Leaning closer, he nipped at her collarbone, enjoying the sprinkling of chill bumps that the contact brought to a usually ignored spot. He was just about to see what her ear lobe thought of attention when she pushed him away.

"Let me talk, Ty."

"Okay."

"Wes was a product of—" she closed her eyes "—of unprotected sex."

Why was she bringing that up? Then it hit him. "You're not on the Pill?"

"I told you it's been some time."

"I know you did," Ty murmured as he realized he'd been no better than an eager seventeen-year-old, all reason neatly bypassing his brain in search of immediate gratification. "I didn't even think."

A hint of a smile entered her expression. "I didn't, either."

He was a doctor. He didn't need lots of excuses or words of wisdom. He knew what they'd done and the possible side effects. "Are you worried?"

"Not really. The thought just occurred to me. I'm pretty sure it's not the right time of the month."

"Then I won't worry, either." Tenderly, he ran a hand down her spine, taking care not to neglect the base of her back. He loved how her skin felt next to his, soft, like a baby's skin. The way she felt so right against him, all pliable curves and pale, creamy softness. Some kind of lotion or powder on her skin smelled faintly of lemon or flowers. Fresh, sweet. Like her.

"So…what do you want to do now?"

She kissed him, giving Ty all the answer he needed. He'd just leaned closer, ready to tell her he would run out to get something when Claire sat up with a start, shock sliding across her face. "Oh, my gosh, Ty. What happened? My son is down the hall."

He had no answer. "Life?"

After a long moment, she nodded. "I think that just about sums it up." She scrambled out of bed. Ty got a quick glimpse of her pretty pale skin, all five-foot-two of her, before she hurriedly threw on a pair of shapeless sweats. "I'm going to go make up the couch."

He new better than to consider asking her to stay next to him. "I'll sleep there, Claire."

"No, I will. There'll be less to explain that way. And I promise you, I'm in no hurry to explain any of this."

He wasn't, either. "I'll help you get the sheets."

Silently, they made up the couch. Ty pulled her into his arms and kissed her before they separated. When she tried to pull away, he shook his head. "If Wes sees this, I'm not going to apologize. I like you, Claire. I find you attractive. I like kissing you. There's nothing wrong with that."

And just to make sure she believed him, he held her close and kissed her again. To his pleasure, she responded wholeheartedly, wrapping her arms around his neck, leaning into him. Brushing her breasts against his chest. Within seconds, their hips touched, too.

And he couldn't help it, his body reacted. "Want to come to my bed again? Before you sleep on the sofa?"

"What I want and what I have to do are two different things."

"Which one is winning right now?"

"Responsibility. I'm sorry."

"Me, too."

"Good night, Ty."

He squeezed her hand right before letting it fall. "Good night."

Then he walked back to his own bed, which suddenly seemed a little bigger than he remembered. Wearily, he punched a pillow. Rolled over.

Smelled her scent.

Sank into oblivion.

Chapter Twelve

"So you survived okay in the storm?" Lynette asked, her hands curved around her fourth or fifth cup of coffee. On Monday morning, Lane's End was blessed with a healthy dose of bright sun, making the streets and lawns look crisp and inviting and almost like a Colorado winter.

"We did." Claire had bundled up in her favorite brown corduroys, cream turtleneck sweater, and thick-soled boots and thankfully made it into work without a problem. Sometimes the snow and ice removal was a catch-can thing.

Their supervisor had given her and Lynette the same break for once, and they were enjoying the relatively rare occurrence by drinking too much coffee and eating doughnuts that one of the nurses on staff had brought in honor of a birthday.

Lynette picked out a coconut-covered doughnut and bit in, her expression pure bliss before she spoke. "We were twenty-eight hours without power at my place. I thought me and Bob were going to become human Popsicles. Even Shady, the cat, cuddled up next to us!"

That was news. Lynette had the meanest cat Claire had ever had the misfortune to meet. "I hope he didn't bite you."

"Only once." After another sip of coffee, she asked, "How long was the power out at your place?"

Claire almost made something up. But she really needed a friend to discuss things with. And, at the moment, they were the only two in the rec room, so things were as private as they could ever be. "I wasn't home. Well, I mean, I didn't get home until early this morning."

"Oh, yeah? Where did you go?"

It was now or never. "I was at Ty Slattery's."

"What?"

Claire winced. "Not so loud! If you start making a scene and someone else hears about this, I'm never going to forgive you."

"I'm not making a scene. I'm just trying to grasp the basics. How in the hell did you end up there?" In a rush, she dropped her doughnut on the table and brushed off her hands. "That must have been some dinner."

"He was supposed to come to my house for baked ziti, so don't act like it was fancy."

"But—"

"Well, when our power went out, I called him to say that I couldn't cook. Next thing I knew, he came over and picked us up."

"Just like that."

Claire snapped her fingers. "Just like that."

"No, I don't think so. There's more going on, isn't there? In between the lines." Studying her a little more closely, Lynette smiled. "This wasn't just a friend thing, was it?"

"It started out that way. The first night, we were all in

sleeping bags in front of the fireplace. Wes and Ty cooked hot dogs. But then he got called in and he asked if I could just stay so he wouldn't have to take me home."

"And you said yes."

"And I said yes. The next day, I cleaned up, hung out with Wes, made stew. Then…something happened." Well, that was one way to describe it, Claire supposed. Something had definitely happened. "You could say that something definitely happened." Actually, Claire still felt that no words could describe the last two days with Ty. Being in his bed had only been part of the bliss. Mostly, she'd just enjoyed his company. Had enjoyed being around him.

To Claire's relief, Lynette didn't looked shocked. Instead, she looked more…reflective. "Hmm. I'm just imagining this, now, but I'm seeing dark, cool rooms. Scary, sit-on-the-edge-of-your-bed ice storms, and being wrapped up in the warm comfort of a handsome man." She paused significantly. "A handsome young man."

- Ouch. He *was* young. Four years younger, still on the other side of thirty, making her feel old. Almost Mrs. Robinson-like.

Seeing that bemused look on Lynette's face turn knowing, Claire tried to refocus the conversation. "It wasn't like that. Picture domestic bliss. Stew. Wes happy and relaxed. A glass of wine."

"Wes and wine? Come on, Claire. No one's that good. Ty Slattery is positively dreamy. Don't tell me there wasn't even a kiss."

Oh, that kiss! Her knees melted, just thinking about the way his lips had sought hers. How for a moment there was really nothing else that mattered except getting a little closer.

Lynette chuckled. "Ha! I knew it. Come on, spill. It's been forever since I thought about kisses."

Claire was just about to set her straight when a voice called out, "Break's over, girls."

Lynette guiltily looked at her Mickey Mouse watch and rubbed the red leather band. "Wow, it is. You'll have to fill me in later."

Claire sighed. For a moment there, she'd been tempted to tell Lynette the whole sordid story, just to share it with someone.

But it actually hadn't been sordid at all. No, it had been sweet and tender. Full of passion. And had left her wanting more.

And more had come right around the corner. If she closed her eyes, in an instant she could feel Ty's arms around her. Bare skin next to bare skin. Old feelings, long ago tamped down, spurred to life.

Even though Ty was wrong for her. Too young. Too busy. Too used to being in charge.

Of course, all of his negatives didn't remove the blame from solidly resting on her shoulders. She'd made a mistake.

Now she was going to have to live with the fact that after all this time of doing her best to get life back on track, she still had no problem with messing things up completely, totally, on her own.

The afternoon flew by. She and Lynette stayed busy, checking in a fairly constant stream of people, updating paperwork and files whenever there was any free time. Lynette clocked out an hour before Claire, much to Claire's relief. Lynette had kept shooting amused glances Claire's way, so much so that even other receptionists were starting to wonder what the deal was.

Three days passed. Ty hadn't called and she hadn't seen him at the hospital, either. But that was okay. She'd been busy at the reception desk, then had been just as busy at home with everything else that had to get done. She helped Wes with homework and did laundry. She ran to the store, the library, cringed at the gas station. She did everything she was supposed to, but still couldn't help but think of Ty, her impulsive night with him and how they hadn't spoken since.

By Friday afternoon, she felt like she'd just been through the longest week of her life. Wes was staying after school for a wrestling practice, so she had until seven to herself. Too much time to sit and stew and worry. Nothing was on television, no book grabbed her attention.

Her four walls were starting to feel confining.

Taking a risk, she called her friend Tessa.

Tessa answered on the first ring. "Hey, Claire! This is a nice surprise. How are you?"

"I'm okay."

Immediately, concern filled her tone. "You sure? You don't sound like it."

"Actually, I'm not okay, if you want to know the truth."

"Is it Wes? Your job?"

"No, it's nothing to do with Wes. He's great and doing really well in his classes." Remembering how Tessa had helped her with her work and sorting out her life, she added, "Work's good, too."

"Then it's got to be something personal. Am I right?"

"You're right." Taking a risk, Claire said, "I did something really stupid the other night."

"This sounds like we need pizza. Want to meet me at the Works?"

"You don't mind coming all the way out to Lane's End?"

"Nope. Keaton's on third shift tonight, so he won't be home for a while. Can you meet me in an hour?"

HUGGING TESSA PHILLIPS was always like coming home, but to a home Claire had never really known until recently. Perhaps it was the good memories Tessa brought— memories of finally seeing a future for herself and Wes that didn't involve hunger or fear.

The pizzeria, located in a renovated train station in downtown Lane's End, was noisy and fun. The walls were lined with vintage train memorabilia, and a huge brick oven took center stage, allowing patrons to watch their pizzas getting cooked.

"It's good to see you," Claire said, meaning every word.

Tessa nodded happily. "It's been forever since we've gotten together," she commented as they were shown to their spot, a sturdy antique oak table covered with a variety of stickers naming tourist destinations. "Where does the time go?"

"You tell me. It feels like just the other day we were planning your trip with Wes."

"Taking him to Disney World was the highlight of last summer for Keaton and me. So, how's he doing?"

Claire filled Tessa in on Wes's wrestling and schoolwork in between ordering a pepperoni pizza and a glass of merlot.

"And your job?"

Dutifully, Claire talked some more, nonchalantly rubbing her fingers over a See Rock City sticker on their table. She shared a few stories about Lynette and a new promotion she was considering applying for. Next they dove into the pizza while Tessa talked about Keaton and her work at Designs for Success.

And then, Tessa leveled a look at Claire. "Okay. We can't put it off any longer. What's going on?"

"I met someone."

Pure pleasure lit Tessa's eyes. "It's about time! Okay, who is he? What's his name?"

Claire answered the easiest question first. "Ty Slattery. He's a resident at Lane's End Memorial."

"A doctor. Did you meet him at the hospital?"

Claire really appreciated how Tessa didn't act the least bit surprised that someone with such an occupation would be interested in someone who'd only taken a few classes in the local community college. "I did. I'd seen him around, but then one afternoon we both took care of a patient together."

"And everything fell into place." After looking longingly at the last piece of pizza on the tray, Tessa pushed her plate away. "That's kind of how it went with Keaton and me, though we thought we were complete opposites."

"That's how it is with Ty and me. He's had a pretty full life, with college in Michigan, then medical school, and now he's finishing up his residency. I've been married, then divorced. I have a child. He's a doctor, I'm a glorified receptionist."

"What about things that matter? Does he like kids?"

"He loves them. He helps out with the wrestling squad. He's been great with Wes. When we spent the night with him, Ty really took Wes under his wing."

"Hold on." In a complete about-face, Tessa pulled back her plate, grabbed the remaining slice of pizza and dug in. Around her second bite, she murmured, "Tell me about staying over at Ty's."

"It's not like it sounds. My place was freezing during the ice storm and we already had a date scheduled. It just seemed like the right thing to do, to be someplace warmer to ride out the storm."

"Because of Wes."

"Right." Claire grabbed hold of that excuse like the proverbial lifeline. "I didn't want Wes to get sick."

Tessa's lips twitched. "That would be terrible."

"I cannot believe you're making a joke out of this!"

"And I cannot believe you're trying to tell me that you spent the night with a gorgeous man who you like, solely for the welfare of your son. Such self-sacrifice!"

Put that way, Claire had to admit that her excuses did sound a little ridiculous. "There was more to my wanting to be there than just Wes. A lot more."

"Ooohkkay...." Tessa sipped from her glass and drummed her fingers. "Anytime you want to actually tell me what happened, I'm all ears."

Claire felt herself blushing. "I guess I'm giving you information in tiny little snippets, huh?"

"Well, let's just say at this rate, we'll be here all night by the time you get to the good stuff."

Tessa's dig made Claire look at her watch, which in turn made her jump up. "Shoot. Wes is going to be done with his practice in thirty minutes. We don't have time to go through this now."

But Tessa didn't take that bait. Instead, she laid a hand

on her arm. "Claire? What is going on? What is it that happened that you're not telling me?"

Leaning forward, she finally came clean. "I slept with him."

For the first time, Tessa looked at a loss for words. "Oh."

"I know! It was so unlike me! At least, I thought it was."

"Hey! Claire, I'm not judging you, I'm just surprised."

"I'm kind of surprised by the whole thing, too."

"So, was it good?" Pure amusement entered Tessa's eyes, letting Claire know that maybe Tessa had been in the same kind of situation once before.

"Yes, actually." Boy, that was putting it mildly! "But we never used protection."

A silky-soft smile spread across Tessa's patrician features. "That must have been some night."

"It was, I mean I think it was. We haven't talked since."

"Not even at the hospital?"

"No. Maybe he's avoiding me." Claire hated to think that, though.

"You two need to talk."

"We will." Sometime.

"No, I mean you two need to talk, soon." Eyes lighting up, she said, "Hey, how about I have Wes tonight? I'll pick him up and take him through a drive-through. We'll get movies, too."

"Are you sure? He's going to need clothes and stuff." Claire couldn't help but notice that she was focusing on logistics instead of reasons why she shouldn't take Tessa up on her offer.

"That's easily taken care of. Do you mind if we stop by your place?"

"Of course not."

"Then it's no problem. Tell me again where the school is and I'll go get him."

Before she knew it, Tessa was gone, ready to take care of her son, leaving Claire to make the slow walk to her car, where she'd promised she'd make a phone call to Ty.

Chapter Thirteen

Ty was freaking out. It wasn't a good thing. He liked being in control. He liked knowing what he was getting into and weighing the pros and cons of any situation. So this batch of anxiety was hitting him hard—especially since it all had to do with Claire.

He couldn't stop thinking about her—and that scared him half to death. Yes, he'd been attracted to her, but he hadn't intended to become consumed. What was it about that woman that was keeping him up at nights?

It wasn't the sex. Well, maybe it was. Making love with her had been good. Memorable. But it had been more than that. Being with her had felt easy and natural. He liked her body. Liked that it wasn't perfect, because his wasn't, either. He liked her reaction when he'd touched her with gentleness. He liked how things between them had been passionate, too.

But in spite of all that—or maybe because of it—he hadn't called. He'd even done his best to avoid her at the hospital. That had been a mistake. She was most likely confused and hurt by his hot and cold manner.

He just wasn't used to feeling so…smitten. He had a plan, after all. He was going to finish his residency, then get a good job and start the long, painful process of digging himself out of debt. None of those plans had ever included starting a serious relationship.

He just about choked on a chunk of red delicious apple when she appeared at his door. "Claire. Hi."

When he finally caught his breath, she spoke. "Hi. I'm sorry I didn't call first. But I…." She shrugged.

He stepped aside to let her in. "It's good to see you."

"Is it?" To his surprise, she immediately took off her coat and sat down right where they'd watched the episode of CSI on Sunday night. "We need to talk."

Well, there went his next idea of easing into things. Of trying to come up with a decent excuse about why he hadn't called the past week. "Okay."

"About the other night—"

He cut her off. "I'm not going to apologize for making love, Claire. Things might have happened fast between us, but I'm not sorry they did."

She blinked. "That's it?"

Now he was really confused. What had she been hoping he'd say? "That's all I've got, Claire. What are you worried about?"

"Us, and our future. And, well, maybe of being pregnant."

He sat down, too. Sure this had been the first time in a while that he'd had sex without protection. But there had been a few other times in the past. "Don't you think you're over-reacting a little? I mean, I don't think my fifth grade teacher was right. Girls don't always get pregnant from one time."

"I know that." She stood up and picked up her coat.

"Listen, I'm sorry I came over. I don't know why I did. I got all caught up in my friend Tessa's advice and didn't think things through. That's so not like me."

He couldn't help but chuckle. "I was just thinking those same things—about myself." It was time for honesty, even if the honest truth was hard to say. "I haven't been avoiding you because I was worried about a baby. I've been thinking about our future, too."

"And?"

"I just realized that you mean a lot to me. If you want to know the truth—I wasn't planning on that. It scared me a little."

Claire's eyes shone with unshed tears. "Really?"

"I do like you. Very much. How about if we just back up and take things slow? We don't have to plan a lifetime."

"Maybe just a few dates?"

"Well…yes. I'm not ready to get serious, and you aren't, either. But I like your company. I really do."

"I like yours, too."

"And, well, I'm not great relationship material anyway. I've got to concentrate on finding a job. I owe so much money, it's not funny."

Claire sat back down, right on top of her coat that had just fallen from her hands. "What?"

"Medical school's not cheap, as I'm sure you know. I owe over a hundred grand."

She paled. "I had no idea."

"Well, you weren't supposed to. It's not something I'm in any hurry to broadcast."

"But aren't you worried? If I had those debts, I'd have an ulcer, for sure."

"I'm concerned, but not too worried. I'm sure not the only one in debt. Pretty much every doctor leaves medical school owing a small fortune."

"Oh. Well, then. I certainly can see why you aren't looking for anything serious."

"So, where's Wes? Do we need to go get him?"

"No, Tessa picked him up and is having him spend the night with her."

"Have you eaten dinner?"

"We went to the Works and had too much pizza."

"I've overindulged there a time or two myself." Concentrating on keeping things nice and easy, he remembered the allure of the movie theater. Dark, cool, not having to talk too much, but at the same time, able to enjoy just knowing the girl you liked was sitting beside you and would maybe hold your hand. "Do you like movies?"

"I love movies."

"Well, let's go to one." He winked and appreciated the shy, sweet smile she flashed back his way. "It's date night."

THE THEATER WAS CROWDED though not packed, but it still made picking a pair of seats a little difficult. They finally decided to sit about midway up on the end of a row. "I'm glad you don't mind sitting here. My beeper's gone off too many times to take a chance on disturbing a whole row of people."

"Are you on call now?"

"No, but…" He shrugged, recalling too many patients to name that he'd given his pager number to, just in case. And though he hadn't known any of them to take advantage, things happened. He was needed, and that was worth everything.

"I understand," she said with a smile.

"You know what's funny? I think you really do."

"I do work in the hospital. And I've started to understand just how dedicated you are." She placed a slim, cool hand on his arm when he tried to come up with something to say to that. "It's a compliment."

As the lights dimmed and the movie trailers came up, Ty slowly maneuvered her hand down his arm, finally linking their fingers together.

Afterward, they walked to the car. "Where do you want to go?" Ty asked.

"Would you mind taking me home?"

He was disappointed, he couldn't deny it. He'd been hoping for another long night together—this time without a thirteen-year-old down the hall. But he also recalled his earlier words. To take things slow. "I wouldn't mind at all."

Ty held her hand as they drove through the dark streets of Lane's End. Later, he walked her up the stairs to her apartment and kissed her good night. Things between them were good. That was enough.

TWO WEEKS LATER, Ty wished he felt relaxed and at ease. He was helping out at the Tristate Invitationals and everything that could go wrong had. The meet had lasted all day, with some wrestlers competing five or six times. By seven o'clock that night, everyone was tired and mistakes were being made.

It was all he could do to keep his mouth shut as he shifted uncomfortably on the wooden bleachers as the coaches yelled out commands and corrections to their wrestlers. The day wasn't Lane's End's finest; one wrestler after another lost his match.

Behind him, he could feel Claire tensing up as Wes warmed up with the jump rope. Wes, all of 103 pounds, was then called to the match and circled his opponent.

Then it all happened fast. His opponent kicked out a leg, wrapped it around Wes's ankle, and he fell, fast. Before Wes could scramble out of it, the other boy twisted an arm and pinned his shoulder. Wes's face turned white.

Claire gasped behind him.

The minute the ref called time, both the coaches and Ty stood up and approached. But Ty had to give it to the kid, he picked himself up, obviously in pain, walked to the coaches from the other team, shook hands, then walked to Lane's End staff.

Coach Davidson studied Wes carefully. "You hurt, Grant?"

"A little."

"Doc? You want to come on over here?" The coach waved Ty over.

"You bet."

"I'm okay," Wes said.

"I'll just double-check." Motioning to an area a little away from the mats, Ty said, "Come over here, Wes. Let's get out of the way."

From the bleachers, Claire called out. "Wes?"

Wes groaned.

Ty knew the boy didn't want the whole team to see his mom fussing over him, but at the same time it was very obvious that Claire was concerned. "I'm going to take a look at him," he said, doing his best to sound matter of fact and not overly tender.

"Should I come over there?"

Wes glared. "No."

"Want to try that again, Wes?"

"I mean, I'm fine, Mom." Wes bit out.

Standing in front of him, Ty helped Wes pull down the top of his singlet. The boy's shoulder was a little swollen, but nothing looked out of place. "I think we'll ice you up and tell the coach you're done for the day."

"No way—"

Lowering his voice, Ty said, "I care about you, Wes. If I thought you were fine, I'd let you know."

Wes met Ty's gaze. In his eyes was a flicker of burgeoning trust that made Ty feel both joy and a weight of responsibility. No matter what was happening between himself and Claire, he and Wes Grant were slowly coming to a new stage in their relationship. "Okay," he said.

A rush of emotion poured on through. Ty was tempted to say something meaningful, but it wasn't the place and he didn't have the words. "Great. I'll go tell Coach Davidson."

THEY ENDED UP going back to Ty's later that night. After reacquainting himself with Maisy, Wes asked if he could roll up some more change while Ty and Claire made a quick spaghetti dinner.

Later, just before Claire and Wes prepared to leave and go home, Ty pointed to the pile of rolled coins on the table. "So, how much do we have now?"

"Almost two hundred dollars," Wes said triumphantly.

Ty whistled low. "That's a lot of dog toys for Maisy."

"That's stupid! You can't spend all this money on dog bones."

"Oh, yeah? What would you spend it on?"

"An iPod."

"How much are those?"

"I saw an ad in Sunday's paper. They've got one for sale for $150."

"Wes, it's time to leave," Claire interrupted.

Ty knew her tone—she didn't like Wes talking about his wants. But he also knew what it was like to do without. Cutting Claire off neatly, he rolled his palm over the stack of coins. "I'd say we have just about that much. You don't have school tomorrow, how about you and I go get it tonight?"

Wes stilled. "What?"

"If we hurry, we can get there before the stores close. What do you think?"

"I think there's a whole lot of other things to spend your hard-earned money on," Claire said. She sent a look his way.

"I don't think so," Ty said, staring at Wes. Honestly, he looked like it was his birthday, Christmas and Easter, all at the same time. "Right now I can't think of a better use for that money. Grab a sack, Wes."

With a screech, Wes's chair slid back against the wood floor. Claire whipped out a hand and stilled his progress. "What are you doing, Ty?"

"Going shopping. Want to come?"

"No. And, Wes, you can't go, either. You can't accept such a gift." Wes glared but sat back down.

That obedience sealed the deal for Ty. Wes was a good kid. But he'd also gone without a lot of extras. Letting that boy spend his change on something he'd really wanted made Ty feel good. "Every once in a while you've got to do something that doesn't make sense, Claire." He hoped she was remembering their night together. Sometimes, being impulsive was a good thing.

But she wasn't budging. "Ty, I can't let you do this."

"It's just an iPod, Mom."

"I told you, we'd think about getting it for Christmas."

As Wes folded his arms over his chest and Claire's cheeks turned pink, Ty interrupted. "It's my gift. My decision. Okay?"

Claire shook her head. "You've got bills."

"Wes, go take Maisy outside for a moment, would you?" As soon as they were alone, Ty said, "This money is not going to make a dent in my bills. And I'm not trying to buy his affection, if that's what is bothering you. I'm just trying to do something nice. I planned to let Wes have the money from the moment I handed him the paper rolls. Let me."

"You should have spoken to me about this."

"It's just forgotten change, Claire. Come on, don't spoil this."

They heard Wes stomping his feet outside the door. "All right," she said reluctantly, "but I want you to know I don't agree with any of this."

"I understand."

"I hope you do, Ty. I really hope you do."

Chapter Fourteen

They were alone again, just she and Wes. Just like they used to be. Well, except that she now had the radio to herself because Wes had tiny headphones in his ears.

After the trip to the electronics store, Ty and Wes had camped out on Ty's computer, learning how to download songs and work that little gadget. Claire did her best to pretend she couldn't care less about it, but she did have to admit that the thing was pretty neat.

Not that she was in any hurry to admit that out loud.

No, she'd much rather concentrate on being mad. Claire wasn't sure which she was more upset about—that Ty was giving Wes something she wasn't able to afford or that he did it all without asking her permission.

Then there was the whole business about spending money on frivolous things. Why wasn't he more concerned about saving money?

He owed a hundred thousand dollars!

His total ambivalence about it reminded her too much of Ray, which of course reminded her of the painful day when she'd realized that she couldn't pay her rent. A hundred dollars would have come in real handy, then.

"I'm hungry, Mom."

With some surprise, Claire saw that Wes had put his new gift away. "McDonald's sound good?"

"It always sounds good."

Oh, how often had they had this conversation? "Well, at least some things are still the same." Claire smiled as she turned right at the next intersection and pulled into the drive thru. "The usual?"

There was that familiar smile. "Yeah."

"One Big Mac combo and one Coke," she said into the speaker.

"Aren't you going to eat?"

After getting her total, she pulled forward in line. "I'm still full from dinner." Only a teenage boy could eat so much!

"You know, you shouldn't have gotten so mad."

Obviously her attempt to hide her feelings hadn't been very successful. "That's easy for you to say. You got what you wanted."

"It wasn't like that, Mom. I didn't ask Ty to buy anything. You know that."

He was right, but that still didn't make things better. Did it?

Thinking about how easily Wes had taken the money from Ty, she said, "You know, you can't expect more things like this from him." She paid the cashier, then after receiving the food, handed it to Wes. "Ty's not made of money."

The easy relaxed tone disappeared in a flash. "Why are you being like this? It was just a gift."

"Which you took."

"You've taken gifts without acting like a witch."

Because his snippy voice implied a much worse word, Claire struggled to keep her voice even. "Such as?"

His chin went up. "You know."

"No, I don't." Before she turned left, she glanced at Wes again. At her son who still hadn't so much as opened that meal that had cost five dollars. Then realization hit. "Are you talking about when we were homeless?"

"Maybe."

"That was different."

"Not really. Oh, Mom, did you have to be so mean? Ty was just being nice. You've ruined everything."

And with that, in went the ear plugs and on went the iPod.

Claire's hands shook. Silently she drove and replayed the conversation while beside her Wes digested his burger with gusto. Once she parked, Wes gathered his things, tromped up the apartment stairs, and used his key to let himself in.

She followed.

Inside, Wes stomped to his room and shut his door behind him with a defiant slam.

Claire only made it as far as the kitchen table before giving in to exhaustion. Yes, she'd taken a lot from other people when they'd been homeless. She'd let Tessa and Keaton pay for Wes's clothes and school supplies. She'd accepted free clothes. She'd gratefully eaten food she hadn't paid for at the shelter.

No, accepting food and clothing wasn't the same as accepting a pricey toy. Claire was shocked to realize the donations had made an impression on Wes.

She'd handled everything pretty badly that evening. Just when she was contemplating going to bed, the phone rang.

She glared at the caller ID before picking the receiver up. "Ty?"

"Hey. Are you still mad at me?"

"Yes. I mean, I don't know. Actually, I think I'm mad at myself. I made too much of everything. And, well, I forgot about being the recipient of some pretty nice gifts myself." Briefly, she filled him in on their trip to McDonald's and the words that were exchanged.

Ty was quiet a moment. "I'm sorry. I wasn't thinking."

No, he hadn't. But maybe she hadn't thought through a lot of things, either. "I'm sorry, too." Eager to make peace, she said, "I'm glad you called."

"Listen, I also wanted to ask you something. Three weeks from now is a dance at the VFW Hall. I've got to go. There's some guys who will be there—guys recently home from Iraq. I want to go show my support. If I promise not to buy Wes another thing without asking you first… would you want to go with me?"

He sounded so cute. And, well, she didn't want to be mad at him forever. "I'd like that."

"Really? Wow. That was easy."

Claire smiled, because she could almost hear the smile in his voice. "I like veterans. And a dance sounds fun. The only hiccup would be if something happened with Wes, like a commitment I had to do with him or if he was sick." She added those things because she wasn't sure if he had any idea about what it was like to be a single mom. Her needs always came behind her son's. And sometimes plans had to be broken on the spur of the moment.

Not that she had an exciting social life or anything.

"Would you like me to hire a babysitter for you? I've

got a good friend who has a teenager who's always looking for a job."

Claire winced. She could just imagine how that little scenario would go over. Wes would see a teenage girl and either become embarrassed about their little place, or embarrassed because she was getting paid to be near him. Either way, he'd take it out on his mom. "I'll see if he can spend the night at a friend's house."

After another few minutes of conversation, she fought a yawn. "I better go. I'll see you at the hospital on Monday."

"I'll come find you. Call me tomorrow if you want."

"I just might," she said before they hung up and Claire went right to bed. However, sleep was hard to come by, there were too many things on her mind.

Too many memories. She leaned back in the pillows and tried to count her blessings. Funny how when things were worse, it used to be easier. At one time having a pillow beneath her head was cause for a celebration. Now she had four and it didn't seem enough.

She didn't know whether to feel embarrassed that things were so good or sad that she'd forgotten to be grateful.

Chapter Fifteen

Maisy barked happily in the park behind Ty's house. As he let the lead out, allowing Maisy freedom to explore an empty robin's nest and the surrounding bushes, Ty thought a lot about Wes and the bond they'd begun to develop.

He'd seen Wes at school just that afternoon when he'd stopped in to get some information from the coach. Wes was sitting off to the side, looking ticked that he wasn't able to participate a hundred percent. Obviously the news that his shoulder was doing a lot better hadn't impressed him much.

Who could blame him? Back when Ty was a teen, he'd only been thinking about his immediate future, not about things that were days and weeks away.

Maisy barked again, bringing Ty back to the present. With a tug, she pulled on her leash, bringing him straight over to his neighbor two blocks over, Cary Hudson. Cary was a popular high school algebra teacher at Lane's End High. Just a few months ago, he'd gotten married to Gen, a Lane's End police officer.

Ty had had the opportunity to work with both of them through the last year, once with Gen during a case of domestic disturbance and another time with Cary when he was helping out at school.

Cary sauntered over with his two beagles Sadie and Sludge. "Long time, no see, Ty. What's been keeping you?"

"The weather. It's been too damn cold for me to take Maisy out for more than ten minutes. The ice hasn't helped."

"I feel the same way. We haven't walked much, either, and now we're all out of shape." Cary pointed to one of the beagles, who was already lying down and looked eager to stay there for some time. "I think Sludge could spend every day on the couch, with frequent potty breaks. Sadie here, is Gen's dog all the way. She's happiest out in the elements."

"How's Gen?"

"Good. Keeping busy. That ice storm kept her out all night and most of the next two days. I almost felt bad sleeping in during my snow days while she was working so hard." He shook his head. "You should hear her stories about the idiot drivers."

Ty laughed. "She wouldn't need to, I probably treated half of them. Luckily, I didn't have to go in until Sunday. But it was crazy at the hospital. I'm surprised Gen and my paths didn't cross once or twice."

Cary petted one of the beagles. "I'll tell her you said hi. Maybe we can do something, the three of us, soon."

"It would have to be four or five, now."

"What?"

"I'm dating someone. She's got a kid. A thirteen-year-old boy."

"Hey, good for you." Cary stood up. "A woman and her son, huh? How's that going?"

"I'm not sure. It's just that, well…we've gotten pretty

close, pretty fast. I hope we're not making a mistake by rushing things."

"I couldn't even begin to give you advice. Gen would smack me upside the head if I tried." His dogs howled, then noses touched the ground and tails stuck out. "Oops. I think they just spied a rabbit. Gotta go."

"See you," Ty called out, glad Maisy was too old to go chasing rabbits. As they walked back home, Ty wondered what was going on between him and Claire. Had going to bed really been as unintentional and spur of the moment as he'd originally thought?

Or were there other factors at work? Was he once again trying to grab hold of a future to carry out a set of dreams he wasn't entirely sure would happen?

Or maybe once again he was thinking about things too much. It sure as hell wouldn't be the first time.

"YOU GOING TO BE OKAY without me?"

That obstinate look that Wes was perfecting made its now regularly scheduled appearance on his face. "Mom. I'm going to be with Tessa. Not that I needed to be."

"I'm sorry your buddy had to cancel on you at the last minute. I know you were looking forward to spending the night with him."

"I could've stayed home alone. I would've been just fine."

With supreme effort, Claire refrained from saying that he was way too young to be even thinking about spending the evening alone in their apartment complex. Yes, it was safer than a lot of other places they'd lived, but there were still dangers. Still a lot of people who she didn't know.

But saying all that would have just ignited another minor

war. "You know how much Tessa and Keaton like having you with them. Tessa's always asking when you can come over."

"I feel like a baby."

"We both know you're not. You could take care of yourself and anyone else who comes along. But, can you just let them take you out without another argument?"

Grudgingly, Wes said, "Keaton said we were going to go to Game, Set, Match."

The arcade restaurant was his favorite. "That sounds like fun."

"I told them we didn't need to go. I know it's expensive. And we just went for my birthday."

Not wanting to get into another argument about expensive gifts, she merely said, "I think they like to go to that restaurant. There's not too many places where you get to have so much fun playing arcade games. Be sure you remember to say thank you."

"Oh, Mom."

Before they could launch into yet another round of discussions about her manners and his lack of them, Tessa pulled up in her BMW. Not wanting to make Tessa get out of the car or get grilled about her upcoming date, Claire opened the front door and waved Wes out. "Go on so you two can get on your way."

Wes looked just as eager to say goodbye. He waved to Tessa, then sauntered to the car, all his things in a stuffed backpack slung over one shoulder. Now it was time to put on her dancing shoes.

"YOU LOOK PRETTY, Claire."

Ty's voice was husky and appreciative. He made her feel like a million dollars in her old basic black dress.

He, on the other hand, definitely did look priceless. In fact, he looked every inch of the successful doctor he was. Well, would be one day, Claire was certain. Dressed in a navy blue suit with a lapis-blue tie, he was handsome and striking. His eyes looked bluer than ever.

As they walked to his car, she commented on it. "Your body must know you're about to be near other soldiers. You suddenly look like you just stepped out of that life."

He laughed. "Sometimes it does feel that way, I don't know why. Maybe it's because I've got friends over in Iraq. Every time I think of them, I want to stand a little straighter…be more like them."

His answer surprised her—of course, so many things about Ty did. Just when she thought she had him figured out, he showed yet another side and she was again reminded that he was so much more than just an up-and-coming doctor. "How did you get involved with so many guys in the army? I can't imagine you met too many of them in medical school."

Ty seemed to weigh his answer before replying. "Chris and I were buddies with some guys who enlisted right after high school and are still in. We've stayed close and helped them when we can. Chris has gotten involved with a lot of USO type of stuff in the Cincinnati area. He's encouraged me to help out when I can. I've gotten donations from hospitals and volunteered when they've asked. These men and women are worth it, you know?"

Claire reached out and squeezed his hand. "I know. I'm looking forward to meeting them. And Chris."

"You'll like him and his wife. And you'll see what I mean when you get a chance to meet these soldiers. Each man and woman is pretty cool. Together, they're something else. I envy their being a part of a group who work together to mean something. To make a difference."

"Medicine's that way."

Once again Ty paused before answering. "Doctors aren't all that different from other professionals, I'm afraid. There's all types. And, like any other job, there's some days when you just don't want to be there."

"It's got to be the same with the army."

He chuckled. "Yeah, but in the army, I'm pretty sure they tell you how to think. At least, that's what a few of the guys have told me time and again."

Darkness had fallen and, for once, it was a fairly clear night. Stars were showing themselves, lighting Claire's spirit. That went a long way, considering that she had a terrible suspicion that her period was late. Her body felt different. More feminine.

Though it might be wishful thinking, Claire hoped her newfound femininity was because of the way Ty made her feel and not from her body getting ready for a baby.

The parking lot was full when they arrived. As Ty slid into a parking space, he looked, for the first time, tentative. "This might be a little different. People get excited and, well, it can get a bit crazy. I hope you're okay with that."

"I can handle it."

There went that grin again. "Don't say I didn't warn you."

Claire instantly understood what Ty meant when she stepped inside. The rather stark, wood-paneled building was decorated to the hilt with banners made of paper and fabric. Red, white and blue balloons tied jauntily to baseball caps decorated the center of each table. "Baseball hats?" she whispered as they hung up their coats in the large coatroom near the entrance.

"That was kind of a joke with some of the guys. They told Chris and me that they talked a lot of baseball out there. You know, like, 'When we get back we're going to watch the Reds, eat popcorn and have a beer.'"

"Just one?"

With difficulty, he kept a straight face. "Or three or four."

This time she was the one who laughed. "I love it. Come on, let's go meet your friends."

They did. It seemed natural for Ty to take her hand and introduce her to one family after another, then to many of the men and women who had just returned.

When Claire met a mom who not only had a son just returning from Iraq but a son the same age as Wes, she went to a corner table and the two of them shared their own special kind of war stories…the kinds of stories that only moms of teenagers and preteens can tell.

Two other moms joined them, each bringing glasses of wine. As the conversation flowed, Claire felt herself relaxing and smiling more easily.

But she was always aware of Ty. Often, they'd trade smiles from across the room. Or she'd hear his laugh, so genuine and appreciative, and she'd lift her head to look at him.

Women around her sent each other knowing glances, obviously catching the looks she and Ty were giving each other.

For once, Claire didn't care what other people were thinking. It felt good to be part of a couple. It felt good to be associated with Ty Slattery as his girlfriend.

"When are you going to dance with your girl, Ty?" Chris asked when they joined her at the punch table. Claire had been introduced to Chris and Beth the moment they'd arrived. Beth looked ready to have her baby any minute, but still managed to look like she was having a ball from her seat at a front table.

The VFW had brought in a deejay and he was playing a medley of songs from the eighties and nineties. About five or six couples were already dancing.

Ty took the plastic cup of punch from her hand. "I don't know. When should we dance, Claire?"

"Whenever you're ready."

Chris chuckled. "You going to make her wait any longer?"

"Not on your life," Ty replied, passing the cup to Chris, then linking his fingers with hers. Claire let him guide her through the groups of people standing around the food tables, and finally onto the makeshift dance floor. As an old Tim McGraw song played, Ty pulled her into his arms.

Instantly, her body went on alert, becoming aware of each point where they touched. Each inch where skin brushed skin.

"I'm having fun," she whispered into his ear.

He responded by kissing her cheek. "I'm glad. I wasn't sure you were ready for this…it's such a crazy mix of formal attire and a potluck supper."

"I like it. I fit in."

"Why wouldn't you? You're sweet and lovely. I never had a doubt about you fitting in. I was just worried that it might be kind of overwhelming. I'm sorry we haven't spent too much time together."

"It's okay. I've enjoyed watching you. It's nice to see you smile."

"I think this is the first time we've done anything close to a real 'date.'"

"I think you're right."

George Strait's voice rang true and strong, weeping out a melody that encouraged all the dancers to sway a little closer together. Claire and Ty were no exception. As if she'd done it all her life, she looped her arms around Ty's. His hands held her waist securely. The bare skin of her chest brushed against his starched shirt.

Someone dimmed the lights.

And then, like teenagers at prom, they kissed. Kissed some more. Her body felt warm. Liquid. Memories of being wrapped in his arms, with a lot less on, came flooding back.

Suddenly, the room was too bright, too crowded, too noisy. She wished they were alone.

Ty's hips brushed hers, letting her know he was just as affected by their kisses as she was.

Luckily, Big and Rich clamored on next, the lively, raucous music effectively pulling them apart. Ty looked sorry to see her go. "So…more punch? A beer?"

"Anything sounds good." Claire was just about to follow him to the beverage table when she heard the familiar ring of her cell phone in the little evening bag hanging from her wrist. After seeing that the caller was Tessa, she told Ty she was going outside to talk.

"Tessa, is everything okay?" she asked, almost happy to feel the cold air on her face. After that dance, she needed to cool off.

"Oh, it's fine. We had a great time at Game, Set, Match."

Realizing Tessa was calling to say they were on their

way home, Claire struggled to keep her tone upbeat. "Are you all on your way back to Lane's End?"

"Not exactly. We called to ask if you minded very much if we kept Wes overnight. Keaton got a new PlayStation game and, well, he and Wes want to try it out tonight."

"Oh, that's fine." Gosh, did she sound as happy as she felt?

"I figured you might say that," Tessa replied, giving Claire the idea that maybe she hadn't sounded as blasé as she'd attempted to. "Hold on." After whispering to Wes or Keaton, Tessa got back on the line. "Okay, I just got rid of the guys. How's it going?"

"It's going good."

"Having fun?"

"Very much. Ty and I are getting along great."

"I'll call when we're about to leave our house in the morning—just in case you get preoccupied, okay?"

Claire chuckled. If their dance was any indication, being "preoccupied" was definitely in her future. "Thanks." She clicked off, unable to keep from grinning.

From behind her, Ty said, "Is everything all right?"

"Everything's very right." Turning to him, Claire held out a hand. "Wes is going to spend the night with Keaton and Tessa. Something to do with a new video game."

"Thank the good Lord for that." Linking his fingers with hers, he murmured, "So, you're free until tomorrow morning?"

"I am. We are."

"What do you say about lying to everyone? Telling them that it's time to go home?"

She knew what he was asking. She also was very aware

that they had a lot of issues that needed to be resolved and not just put aside.

But, like Wes and his iPod, some things just were too tempting to resist. "Are you sure? I mean, I know how much you wanted to be at the party and see all the guys."

"We did go and I did see the guys." Flashing a smile that reached all the way into her heart, he murmured, "I'm ready to take you home."

They kissed at red lights. Started necking as soon as he parked his vehicle. Claire didn't even bother to pretend that she wasn't eager to go inside with him.

In fact, the only thing that gave her a moment's pause was that her body felt a little different. A little more sensitive.

And though her period was late, there was probably a hundred reasons why that had happened.

As well as the most logical reason of all.

Chapter Sixteen

She couldn't put it off any longer, Claire thought as she stared at the pink line on the pregnancy test. This was the second test she'd taken and, if anything, it had transformed into glorious pink even quicker than the first time.

It was time to face facts. She was pregnant.

"Mom, you ever coming out of the bathroom?"

She quickly put herself back to rights, stuffing the stick back in the box, and then tucking the box in the cabinet under the sink.

Wes knocked on the door again, this time a little too forcefully. Claire pulled open the door with a snap. "What are you doing?"

Her boy glared. "What am *I* doing? You've been in there thirty minutes. What are you doing? Living in there?"

Oh, sometimes she wished she could wash that mouth out with soap. "Yes, Wes. I'm living in the bathroom. My bed's now the tiny bathtub. Why are you so grumpy?"

"I don't know." He looked at the floor. "Is Ty really coming over tonight?"

"He said he was."

"I'm glad you finally forgave him about the iPod."

Claire felt herself blushing. If the night of the dance was indication, she'd forgiven him for any wrongdoing he'd ever done in his life. "Wes, do we really need to bring it up again?"

"Did you forgive him?"

"Yes."

"Are you going to marry him?"

"Marry? What brought this on?"

"You like him, don't you?"

"I do." Her instinct was to say she definitely was not marrying Ty. After Ray, she'd never wanted to marry again. But now, Claire wasn't sure of anything anymore.

"Well, the truth is…I don't know."

"You've been seeing him nonstop. Even the guys at wrestling know that you two are going out. Do you love him?"

His voice was surly and full of teenage drama. But was there a little bit of hope in there, too? "Why don't you take your turn in the bathroom and then we'll talk?"

"I don't need to go."

"You just were being annoying because it's Sunday?"

He turned away. "Never mind."

She could let him walk away. She could keep avoiding his questions, like his concerns didn't really matter. Or, she could face what her conscience was screaming…it was time to talk.

Yes, this baby was hers and Ty's, but she'd had a relationship with Wes even longer. And no one was more important to her than her son. "Listen, I think we probably do need to talk. Why don't you and I go sit down?"

Grudgingly, he approached the couch. Claire followed, then tucked her jeans-clad legs up under her. "Do you want something to drink?"

"No. What do we need to talk about?"

"Something pretty important."

Wes's eyes darted toward the door. "Like?"

Claire had the feeling that not even a year of reading all those self-help books would help this conversation. She went on instinct alone. Prayed that she was doing the right thing. "Wes, the reason it took me so long in the bathroom was because I was taking a pregnancy test."

Right before her eyes, the bottom fell out of her kid's attitude. "What?"

Oh, this was way harder than she would have ever guessed. As Wes's eyes looked like they were about to burn a hole in her stomach, she made herself be stronger. Tougher. What was done was done. Now it was time to stick to the facts.

She needed to concentrate on what she knew and not make any rash proclamations. Soldiering on, she said, "Ty and I made love. And, well, I'm pregnant."

Wes continued to stare at her stomach. Finally he glared at her. "Is this a joke?"

Claire found herself squirming under his incredulous gaze. "I wouldn't joke about something like this. It's a big surprise, I'll tell you that."

"Did you want a baby?"

She didn't know what she wanted. Claire wrapped her arms around herself protectively—even though she knew it was silly. She wasn't seventeen and clueless like she'd been with Ray.

No, now she was thirty-two and clueless. Sheesh! Would she ever learn?

"I want this baby. I mean I will as soon as it sinks in that

I'm going to have one." When Wes still stared at her in shock, she murmured, "I hope when the news sinks in with you, you'll feel the same way."

"Me? I don't want a baby."

Why had she expected hugs and smiles? "It will be your little brother or sister. You've always wanted one of those. Remember?"

Wes grimaced and turned around.

Claire shifted and tried to tell herself that she did not actually have to go to the bathroom again. No, things weren't going well. At all.

Had she actually thought they would?

Breaking the silence, Wes said, "What did Ty say?"

"I haven't told him yet. Or anybody else. You're the first one."

Wes blinked. Claire could almost see him weigh that news with the shocker she'd just zinged him with. "When are you going to tell Ty?"

"Tonight." Even as she said the words, Claire felt her stomach give a little quiver. So much for letting the results sink in and planning what to say. Next thing she knew, she'd be opening the window and telling her whole apartment complex.

"What do you think he'll say? What if he gets mad?" Wes looked genuinely concerned.

Playing it far cooler than she felt, Claire shrugged. "Then I guess he'll be mad."

"What will you do then?"

"I guess I'll take care of you and the baby by myself. We've managed just fine until now, just the two of us, right?"

"Yeah." He sounded doubtful.

Claire didn't blame him. Their life hadn't been easy. But was anyone else's?

When Wes went back to staring at her stomach, Claire spoke again. "I didn't plan on this, Wes. I know Ty didn't. But I'm not unhappy. I'm surprised and scared, but I'm not sad."

Shock played across his features. "You're scared?"

Tears pricked her eyes and Claire prayed her words were going to be able to convey everything she was feeling. "Of course I'm scared. I'm really surprised that I'm pregnant. I didn't think I'd ever have another child. I didn't think I could have more kids."

"Do you think Ty wants kids?"

She saw hope in his eyes. Claire understood in that instant that Wes was wondering if Ty was going to want him, too. That look of hope just about turned her to mush. "I know he likes kids. I know he likes you."

Slowly, Wes nodded.

She rushed on. "We're going to be okay, Wes."

"Even if you're scared?"

"I'm not scared of having a baby to love. I'm scared about taking care of one." With a teasing smile, she said, "You're a big kid. It's been a long time since I had to worry about baby stuff." Just thinking of all the paraphernalia she'd spied in the Wal-Mart aisle the other day made her dizzy. "Diaper Genies. Three-in-one carriers. Baby Einstein! What are those things?"

Before Wes could say a word, she blathered on some more. "Then there's everything that's been going on with you and me."

"Us?"

"Yes, us! It's been just the two of us forever. What if this baby manages to screw up everything that we've got?" She placed a hand on her hip. "And how awful is that? I'm supposed to be excited and thrilled about this baby. Instead I'm scared of how you're going to feel about me. I don't think I'm going to be able to handle it if I've gone and completely disappointed you."

After a moment, Wes shook his head. "I'm not disappointed." After a moment, he smiled slyly. "Not completely."

A weight lifted off her shoulders. "I'm glad. I don't know what I'd do if you were. I think you're a great kid, Wes." She stopped abruptly before she spewed out too many more insecurities. Yet more things that he didn't need to hear about.

Of course, maybe she should have thought about that a good five minutes ago. Before she contracted diarrhea of the mouth.

His arms wrapped around her before she knew what was happening. "It's okay, Mom," he whispered.

Well, that was enough to make her burst into tears. She gripped him hard, rested her head on his shoulder and cried, giving in to waves of frustration and anxiety. And relief. Oh, for heaven's sakes, she was so very, very glad he still cared.

So very glad she hadn't completely messed everything up between them.

Three knocks, followed by the door opening startled them both. Claire didn't know who was more surprised, Ty to find her crying in Wes's arms, Wes to be found that way, or herself, because she was fixating on the fact that he'd just opened the door without waiting to be let in.

After closing the door behind him, Ty came to an abrupt stop, looking in alarm at her and Wes standing together, mascara most likely running down her cheeks. "Claire? Wes? What's wrong?"

Scooting away from Wes, she wiped her eyes, tried to smooth things over. "Nothing's wrong." She summoned a smile. "So…you let yourself in."

"Sorry, I guess I was just impatient to see you. Are you okay?"

She tried to smile. "Maybe."

Wes sat down on the leather recliner. Within seconds, Ty completed the new seating arrangement by taking Wes's place and grabbing both her hands. "Claire? Honey? What's wrong?"

"I'm fine," she hedged. "There's just some things we need to talk about."

Ty's eyes narrowed. "Okay."

From his spot, Wes coughed. "This is even bigger than an iPod."

Ty dropped her hands. "O-kay."

"Well, you see," Claire began, toying with different ways to announce her news.

"Just say it, Mom."

She flashed a look of warning his way. "In a little bit. I think we should let Ty relax first." She turned to Ty. "How about a drink?"

"No, thanks."

"You still have your coat on. How about I take your coat?"

The wrinkle between his brows looked to be deeply embedded. He paused, like he was about to say something, then nodded. "Sure."

She held out her hands, gripped that wool coat with all her might. "I'll put this away. Wes, see what Ty wants to drink."

"Oh, brother," Wes said.

TY'S STOMACH CLENCHED as the charade played out in front of him. Though moments ago he would have been happy with a cup of coffee or a mug of hot chocolate, he suddenly had the need for a drink. Something was up and it wasn't good. "Got any beer, Wes?" He'd asked the question as something of a joke. He'd never seen Claire drink a beer in the time he'd known her.

Instead of grinning, Wes simply went to the fridge and pulled out a bottle of Miller Light. When he handed it over, Ty popped off the cap and had a pull as Wes gestured to the couch. "Mom has something to tell you. Something really important."

He knew. By that tone, by the way Wes was looking at him, like he was part friend and part horrible intruder in their lives, Ty knew. Claire was pregnant.

Claire joined them, hesitating, her hands wrapped around a mug of tea. Those pretty brown eyes looked puffy. Worried. Unsure.

That made him feel like a heel.

Wes knew. Claire knew. He knew. But nobody wanted to say it out loud. Catching her eye, he waited for her to say something. Instead she just sipped her tea.

There was only one thing to do, really—get the gorilla in the room out in the open. "Claire, are you pregnant?"

"Yes."

As Ty took that in, he glanced toward Wes. He looked

like his world had caved in. Claire looked dazed and confused. And he'd caused all this.

He was a doctor. He should have known better.

Now there was only one way to make things right.

It was time to step up and take responsibility. Time to be a man.

If he'd thought it was going to be hard, it wasn't. Actually, it felt almost easy to do the right thing. "We need to get married," he said. "Soon."

"Oh!" Claire's mug of tea went crashing from her hands.

"Wow!" said Wes, right before he looked from his mom to Ty to his mom again.

Ty closed his eyes. *Great marriage proposal, Slattery.*

Chapter Seventeen

Time seemed to stand still. Ty took a swig of his Miller Light and hoped Claire had a couple others stashed away.

Well, that sure as hell wasn't how he'd imagined his first and only proposal would go over. As proposals went, it was pretty damn lame.

Claire wasn't looking at him. In a voice that brooked no argument, she said, "Wes, go to your room."

Instead of obeying, the thirteen-year-old crossed his arms over his chest. "Go to my room? What was all that stuff about how we're in this together? How I'm Mr. Important in your life?"

"That was before Ty got here. Now he and I need to talk. Alone."

"What am I supposed to do in there?"

"I don't care."

"But—"

Claire completely lost it. Holding out a hand, she pointed to her right. "Wes Grant, listen to me! Now. Please! Go!"

Wes narrowed his eyes at Ty before he moved an inch.

"You did this," he muttered before standing up and walking as slow as molasses out of the room.

When the door shut, Claire leaned back and exhaled and finally met his gaze. "I'm sorry. This isn't going quite like I'd hoped it would."

None of this scenario had ever been how he'd imagined it would be, either. But that was all right. Plenty of things had happened in his life that he hadn't counted on.

Still staring into her puffy, teary eyes, Ty tried to grasp how she was feeling. Was she upset about the baby? About him? About his stinky proposal? "So…when did you find out?"

"Over the last few weeks I started feeling really tired. A little queasy. Different. Like I did when I had Wes."

"I didn't know."

"Well, I wasn't sure if I was feeling things because they were really happening or because I was worried that they would." Wearily, she pushed back her hair. "I took a pregnancy test a few days ago. I took another to confirm right before you arrived. I'm positive I'm pregnant, Ty," she blurted. "And, it's your baby."

He couldn't help but be amused. "I know that. I was there, remember?"

Claire's cheeks turned pink. "I remember. I'm sorry. I didn't mean—"

He couldn't stand it any longer. He moved closer and put his arms around her, linking his fingers. "Hush. We knew this could happen. Remember what we said? How we'd deal with this if we needed to?"

"Talking about what might happen is a whole lot different than discussing what really did. I honestly didn't think I could get pregnant."

"I guess you were wrong. I meant what I said, Claire. I think we should get married."

"I'm not ready. I'm not near ready to get married again. Thanks, but no."

To his surprise, the expected burst of relief from hearing those words didn't come. In fact, all he was feeling was irritation. Didn't she even want to consider a future together? Didn't she realize he'd never proposed marriage before? "You don't have to be ready."

"What?"

Oops. There was fire in her eyes. In those sweet, honey brown eyes that looked like they had the patience of the world hidden in their depths. Well, at least the patience of a minor saint. "Claire, I care about you, I'm not going to try and pretend we're madly in love."

"I don't want to pretend anything, Ty." She stood up, glanced toward Wes's door again, as though she was worried he was about to pounce out on them any minute.

Ty wanted to tell her not to worry—Wes probably had his ear at the door and was listening to every word. Ty would. Instead, he did a little pretending. Tried to look happy, assured and relaxed.

Like he got women pregnant and asked them to marry him in front of their teenagers all the time.

Her eyes narrowed.

She probably thought he was a jerk. Hell, he thought he was acting like a jerk. He needed to get a grip on himself, and fast. "If I say some things will you listen?"

"You know I will."

So far, so good. "This baby is a surprise, but not a shock. We don't need to make getting married a bad thing, Claire.

We can plan for the future, plan for the baby...." His voice drifted off, struggling to find the words.

"Plan."

"I do care for you. I care for Wes. I would want to be with you every moment I would even if everything was still the same."

Her eyes softened. "You know, I believe that."

"You should, because it's true."

She reached out to him. He clasped her hand in both of his. Oh, how he loved the way her skin felt, so soft and feminine. Loved how that softness belied the strength that permeated her very soul. Gently, he rubbed his thumb along her knuckles. Smiled when a hint of a shiver raced through her.

She was not immune to him. No matter how she might pretend differently, she was just as aware of him as he was of her. Good.

"Can we not talk about this anymore tonight?" she asked. "Please? Everything's been happening so quickly, I need time to think. So do you. So does Wes."

"Do you want me to stay or go?" He'd do either, but he wanted it to be her decision.

Her lips curved into a watery smile, breaking the intense moment. The several intense moments. "I want you to stay, silly."

"Then I do, too." He looked over at Wes's door. It was still closed, but Ty had a feeling Wes was going crazy on the other side, especially now that he and Claire were almost whispering. "I'm going to go talk to him, if that's okay." Remembering how mad she'd been when he'd taken Wes shopping without her input, he waited a beat. "Is it?"

"It's okay."

As Claire went into the galley kitchen, Ty knocked on Wes's door. He didn't know what, exactly, he was about to say, but he did want to make sure Wes knew that he was important to him. "Wes? Can I come in?"

"Yeah, sure."

The boy's room was small but well thought out. His bed was high in the air, like a top bunk bed. But instead of another bed underneath, there was a dresser, a small desk and a rolling chair. The walls were covered with posters of sports figures and *The Matrix.* A pile of clothes lay on the floor. Ty couldn't tell if they were dirty clothes ready for the washing machine or clean items waiting to be put away.

Wes was sitting on the floor next to a pile of gaming magazines.

He hadn't looked at Ty yet.

Ty closed the door. "How much did you hear?" he asked, sliding down to sit on the floor, too.

"I don't know."

Even though he knew the answer, he asked, "Did you hear me ask your mom to marry me again?"

A moment passed. Wes nodded.

"Did you hear her answer?"

Animosity blazed in his direction. Ty had to give it to Claire, she was one smart mom. Wes was not happy with the situation and obviously needed some time and attention.

And here Ty's gut reaction had been to fix everything in a neat package.

"If you heard, you'd know that she didn't say yes. Actually, uh, I don't know if we're getting married or not. Your mom's thinking about it."

"Are you mad?"

"No."

Wes shoved the magazines aside and faced Ty a little more head-on. "Why not? What did she say?"

"She thinks I'm rushing things. And you know what? She's right." Treading carefully, Ty added, "My knee-jerk reaction to this baby was to try and fix everything. Your mom very sweetly reminded me that there are other factors involved."

"Like what?"

"You. The baby. Jobs. Our histories."

"I can't believe you did that to her," Wes blurted, then stared at Ty with owl eyes, like he couldn't believe he'd voiced what he was thinking.

The blunt statement had shaken Ty, too, but he knew it was no less than he deserved. "I don't know what to say about that. There's not much of an excuse." Well, not one he could share, anyway. No way was he going to tell Claire's kid that he found his mother sexy and pretty as all get-out. That every time he was with her, he just wanted to hold her close and kiss her senseless.

That every time he went to bed at night he remembered how it felt to sleep beside her. To wrap his arms around her and pretend everything was right in the world.

So Ty didn't say anything.

But that was okay, because Wes seemed to have plenty on his mind. "You should have left her alone."

Okay. There it was. Wes wasn't worried so much about the baby as much as his mom doing things no boy wanted to imagine his mom doing.

Well, he had a point about that.

As the silence grew, Ty became aware of other things in

the room. The teenage boy smell…dirty socks and sweat. Interspersed was a faint aroma of Tide…leading Ty to believe that those clothes were clean. Next to his bed were pictures of dogs and puppies. The kid really did want a dog.

And on his desk was a photo of Wes and a very pretty older woman with short dark hair. Both were holding mugs from Game, Set, Match. That gal had to be Tessa.

"I'm not going to excuse my behavior, Wes. But I want you to know a couple of things. Will you listen?"

Wes shrugged.

"Please?"

"Yeah. Whatever."

"I've liked your mom for quite a while, from the first time our paths crossed at the hospital. She's different than a lot of other women I've known. More genuine. Sweeter. When I met you, when I started coaching you, I knew you were pretty great, too."

"You don't have to say all that."

"That's where you're wrong, sport. No matter what happens with me and your mom, I want you to know that I'm glad *we* met. I want to stay friends. Believe me?"

"Is that why you let me spend all your money? Because you wanted to—" he grimaced "—you know, with my mom?"

"No." Reaching out, Ty touched Wes's shoulder until the boy turned to him. "That gift had nothing to do with your mom. Listen, when I was about your age, it was always just me and my dad. Things were hard. My dad—he loved me but he didn't always show it. He didn't have the words. Do you know what I mean?"

Wes nodded. "My friend Tommy's dad is like that. He's tough."

"My dad was tough, too. But one night, he picked me up after I lost a wrestling meet and took me to dinner. An expensive one. Steak. Then, he handed me this stupid leather jacket I'd been wanting."

"What for?"

"I'd seen it at the mall and I really wanted it, but we couldn't afford it. When my dad handed it to me, he said sometimes it's okay to get what you want. That I needed to know that feeling." Ty's throat became thick as he remembered the look of longing in his dad's eyes. Like he'd wished things were different.

"Do you still have that jacket?"

"Nah. It was the ugliest jacket you ever saw, Wes. The next year, everyone moved on to ski jackets and I had to keep wearing my leather one." Ty rolled his eyes. "All I'm saying is that I wanted to give you something. To feel like my dad when he gave me that coat. To let you feel like I did when he held it out to me."

"I like the iPod a lot."

Ty grinned. "I'm glad."

"I'm glad it didn't have anything to do with my mom."

"Me, too." Ty shifted, tried to get comfortable, then realized that goal was futile. Standing up, he walked to Wes's desk and on a notepad wrote his cell phone number. "If you ever need me—or just want to talk—call. Anytime."

"Really?"

"I promise. I'll always be glad you called, Wes." After sharing a look of understanding with the boy, Ty slapped his hands against his thighs. "I bet your mom's probably wondering what happened to us. Maybe we should go out and see her. But first, is there anything else you want to know? Say?"

"Not right now."

"If you ever want to talk again, you'll let me know?"

"Yeah."

His hand on the door, Ty said, "You want to come out and join us?"

"In a few minutes."

As Ty left the room and met Claire's concerned eyes, he hoped he hadn't just made things worse.

Chapter Eighteen

Ten days had passed. True to his word, Ty was giving her time. Unfortunately, Claire wasn't finding the reprieve helpful. If anything, the extra time just made her pregnancy feel more real and daunting.

In lightning speed, her body seemed to wholeheartedly embrace her new condition. Chocolate and apples now sounded really good while scrambled eggs and tuna casserole smelled horrible. Her stomach was in constant upheaval.

Her breasts hurt. She had to pee. And she could hardly wait for bedtime. Two times over the last week, she'd fallen asleep on the couch before ten.

Then, much to her added distress, those sleepy days would be followed by sleepless nights. Hours watching the digital clock tick in neon green. Stressing and fretting over worries that always seemed magnified at three in the morning.

Pretending nothing was different at work. Not even when Ty seemed to take every opportunity to walk by the reception desk and look at her meaningfully.

It didn't help that Wes was handling it all by doing everything in his power to be a jerk. Unfortunately, he was a very good jerk. He complained; he whined. He overslept in the morning and refused to go to sleep at night. Nothing she cooked tasted good, and nothing she said could be listened to without comment.

And he'd just about pushed her to the end of her patience the day before.

"I don't want to go to practice tonight," he announced the moment he got home from school.

"You have to go. You're on the team."

"Not really. My shoulder's sore, remember?"

"I remember. But coach said you were fine. You need to go do your part for the team."

"Maybe I don't want to. Maybe I don't want to wrestle anymore."

"What? You love to wrestle."

"No I don't. I only did it for you."

Well, that was an original spin on things! Yes, Wes was only watching his weight, getting beaten up at matches and swaggering around town in his Lane's End wrestling T-shirts and sweatshirts because his mom wanted him to.

Though she knew he was only pushing her buttons to get a rise out of her, she took the bait. "We both know you are not wrestling for me."

"Yeah, I am! You wanted me to be involved."

"Right. You said no to chess, no to student council and no to the drama club. Out of everything you could have picked to become involved you picked wrestling. All for me."

Only because she happened to see a touch of sadness in his eyes did she attempt to soften her voice. "Wes, you picked wrestling because you like it. You like the boys on the team and the coach."

"Well, I don't anymore. Maybe I'll just go next year. When my shoulder's completely better. When I don't have to work with Ty anymore."

"So you're only saying this because you want to avoid Ty, which is really silly."

Wes's eyes blazed. "What am I going to do when everyone finds out you're pregnant? By him?"

"No one has to know anytime soon. And I don't know what you want me or Ty to say. There's nothing I can do about the past."

"I don't want to talk anymore."

When he picked up the remote control, she braced herself for another round. "You didn't win, Wes. You're still going to wrestling. And since this discussion is so much fun, we should probably talk about your chores, too." Pointing to the pile of laundry on the floor, Claire said, "You were supposed to put those away."

"It doesn't matter. I'll just get them dirty again."

Oh, there had to be a special place in heaven for mothers of thirteen-year-olds. Patience gone, Claire jabbed her finger at him. "Wes Grant, you get your butt up out of that chair and clean up this room. Then, when you do that, you get ready for practice. You're going tonight."

"I don't want—"

"I didn't ask you what you wanted."

"No, you never do anymore," he shot out, right before he turned his back to her and marched off into his room. Just for kicks, he slammed the door.

Her life was a mess. Claire choked back a tear, at a loss of what to do next. At the moment, no child-rearing book seemed appropriate.

No friend came to mind who could offer advice. She was on her own and, for the first time in a long time, Claire felt vulnerable.

When no noise came from Wes's room, Claire decided to give them both a little cooling off time before nagging him again.

Maybe she, too, needed to take a little break. Sit down. Have some tea. Put her feet up.

Her body had other plans. She groaned as a wave of nausea rolled in her stomach. Okay. Maybe she'd sit down right after she rushed to the bathroom and threw up.

And as she finally took a break on the tiny stool in the bathroom, wet washcloth behind her neck, Claire cursed her luck. Unfortunately, child number two had no problem being difficult, either.

"WE HAVE TO STOP meeting like this," Chris Pickett said in the self-checkout line at Kroger the following Wednesday. "Either that or plan to grocery shop together."

Ty smiled at the image. "Yeah, that will be the day. Two guys planning their social life around the sale on aisle five."

"I'd laugh except right now it doesn't sound all that bad. Beth's driving me crazy with this pregnancy. When I'm not painting, I'm shopping for baby crap. When I'm not shopping, I'm getting handed *What To Expect When You're Expecting*."

Ty swallowed hard. "Have you learned anything?"

"Don't even get me started. I now know way more about female anatomy than I ever cared to know. I told Beth I thought I only needed to be there for conception and birth."

"Not everything in between?"

He chuckled. "Maybe for some of it. Truth is, I just don't want to be so well informed. I mean, those days in the fifties with the guys in waiting rooms smoking cigars sound pretty good."

"Yeah, you take out lung cancer and the women delivering by themselves, it was great."

"When I tried to tell Beth that maybe I didn't need to know so much, she handed me a list for the store."

"You want a doctor's advice?"

"Definitely."

"Keep your mouth shut and nod."

Chris slapped his hand against his forehead. "Now you tell me!"

Ty laughed, though inside he felt crushed and inadequate. Chris's days were what *his* life was supposed to be like. What *he* was supposed to be doing. The rush of feelings for Claire and his unborn baby hit him hard and left him feeling more confused than ever.

As they scanned their purchases, Chris said, "So, what have you been doing? Beth asked if you wanted to come over for dinner again soon."

"Even with all the morning sickness?"

"You take her mind off things." Chris grinned. "Shoot, you take my mind off things. Why don't you come over on Sunday night? I think we're having roast."

"Thanks, but I'll probably have plans with Claire."

Chris slipped his credit card in the machine before grabbing his bags and waiting for Ty. "I know you took her to the dance, but are you two serious?"

"We are."

"When did this come about?"

Ty picked up his bags and headed to the exit. "A couple of months ago."

"Well, bring her along for dinner. We'd love to have one more."

"Actually, it would be two more. Claire has a kid."

Chris scrutinized him more closely. "I never thought you'd want to take on a kid."

"Thanks," Ty said sarcastically.

"No, I mean, you've always been so hesitant with relationships since Sharon."

"I'm getting better. Besides, it wasn't a choice, he was just part of the package. I like him a lot. His name's Wes. He's thirteen."

"She has a thirteen-year-old? How old is Claire?"

Ty resented the look Chris was giving him. Like he was in way over his head. "I don't think that's any of your business."

Chris held up his free hand. "Sorry, buddy. I just never thought you'd saddle yourself with an older woman."

Saddle? That was so completely opposite of how he felt about Claire that it took him off guard. "I'm not saddled with anyone." He was in love.

Damn!

Chris eyed him with a new respect as by mutual agreement they headed out to their cars. For once, the temperature was in the forties and the night clear. Ty felt almost warm in his wool coat.

"Hey, Ty. Sorry about the stuff I said. Who you date is none of my business. I'm just glad you're happy. I meant my offer, too. If the three of you want to join us for dinner on Sunday, we'd love to have you."

"Thanks. I'll ask Claire."

"I hope she'll say yes." Slapping Ty's shoulder, Chris nodded. "If you've found someone, I think that's great. I mean it, buddy. I know Beth would love to meet Claire's son."

"I'll call you and let you know."

Ty made a detour on the way home and stopped over at Claire's uninvited. The conversation with Chris had shaken him—not by what he'd said, but by what had been triggered inside him.

He'd fallen, hard. And the knowledge made him eager to move forward.

Wes answered the door. "Hey, Ty," he blurted before seeming to remember that he was avoiding Ty at all costs.

"Hey. Can I come in?"

Wes stepped back, then glanced over his shoulder at Claire, who was standing in the kitchen. When their eyes met, she smiled a greeting. "You came just in time. I'm making cookies."

"What's the occasion?"

"It's Wednesday," she said.

Wes interpreted. "Mom likes to bake, but only when she gets off work early."

"I only work until noon on Wednesdays."

Ty knew that. He knew her whole schedule. He knew she loved to bake. She loved to be home and she never took simple domestic chores for granted.

Even though no one had invited him to, he took off his coat and laid it on the back of the chair, then sat on a stool next to Wes.

Claire hadn't moved from behind the counter. "What brings you here, Ty?"

"I just missed you two."

"Yeah, right." Wes was all sarcasm.

"It's true." Taking a risk, he opened up the door to his past and hoped only a few of his skeletons would pop out at a time. "I didn't do a lot at home, you know. My parents divorced when I was four. After that, it was just me and my dad."

"What happened to your mom?" Wes asked.

"I saw her, but not often and not regularly." Pushing out words he'd never told anyone, Ty said, "I don't really know what happened to her. She, uh, just didn't want to be around anymore. It was just the guys at my house. No cookies."

Wes's eyes widened. Ty hoped he was realizing that maybe everyone else hadn't had a picture-perfect life, either.

Claire lightened the moment. "Well, we've got plenty of cookies here," she said. "That is, if you like peanut butter and chocolate."

Wes pushed the plate over. Obligingly, Ty took one, bit into bliss, then finally decided it was time to speak his mind. He'd never been the type of man to wait for things to happen, and he was frankly getting pretty tired of waiting.

"Claire, Wes, can we talk about things?"

Wes hopped off the stool. "I'll go to my room."

"I'd rather you stayed. If you don't mind."

"Mom?"

Claire shrugged. "I guess we're all in this together."

"Can we get engaged, the three of us?" When they both stared at him like he was speaking Greek, he explained. "I don't know why things happened the way they did. But I think there's a reason for it, and I think it's a good reason. I'd like us to be a family, if you both would be willing to give it a try."

"You'll never be my dad."

When Claire looked about to silence Wes, Ty shook her off. "I know. But maybe we could make things work anyway."

"Where would we live?"

"I was thinking my place, at least for now. I'm just renting it, but there's more space."

"Okay," Wes said. After grabbing another three cookies, he went off to his room.

Ty was grinning until he realized that Claire looked mad enough to toss all that cookie dough at his head. "What are you doing?"

"I'm trying to move forward instead of worrying about the past."

"I'm not ready to get married again."

"Then let's have a long engagement until you are ready."

"You're not going to want to be engaged as long as I would want."

"You don't know that."

"Ty, no offense, but you're the wrong person for me."

"You said I was gorgeous." He'd meant for her to laugh.

"You are. But you're too young."

"I'm only four years younger. Don't treat me like I'm a child."

"You've got a medical practice to begin. You won't want to be weighed down with us."

"Listen to me, Claire. I want you. I want our baby. I want Wes. Now. I'll want all of you ten years from now. I'm not the kind of guy who makes commitments and then leaves."

She bit her lip. "You owe too much money."

"What?"

"I'm scared to death of owing bill collectors. I don't want to be saddled with your loans if something happens to you."

"Nothing's going to happen."

"Everything happens." Her voice turned shrill as she very obviously tried to retain her composure. "Don't you get it? Something *always* happens."

"I'm not going to pretend I won't owe money for a long time. Medical school is expensive. But Claire, one day you're going to have to look forward instead of over your shoulder. One day you're going to have to realize that no man can guarantee to be perfect."

"You're deliberately misunderstanding me."

"You're deliberately putting up roadblocks instead of listening to your feelings." Stepping closer, he said, "Claire, do you love me?"

"I don't know."

"Really?"

Sheepishly, she said, "I think I do."

"I know I love you." After removing the oven mitt from her hand, he linked his fingers through hers. "Can we please be engaged?"

"I don't want to marry until after the baby's born."

"Fine."

"And—"

He kissed her. "Say yes."

"I can't yet."

"What can you say yes to? Dating?"

"I can say yes to dating."

"What about an engagement? A long engagement?"

"Ty—"

"Please Claire? Give us a chance?" Reclaiming her lips,

Ty pulled her close. After a moment's hesitation, Claire responded wholeheartedly, opening her mouth, letting him in. Giving herself freely. Ty wrapped his arms around her and gently rubbed her back. They were both out of breath when they pulled apart.

"I didn't say yes."

"But you're not saying no?"

For the first time, she smiled with true mirth. "I'm not saying no."

Holding her close, he murmured, "I'll take that."

Chapter Nineteen

"Girl, you've got to let me have a shower for you."

Lynette had been giddy with the news from the moment Claire had told her. "A shower is not necessary."

"Of course it is. Not every day a girlfriend of mine catches herself a doctor."

"I didn't 'catch' him. And even if I did, nothing permanent has been settled."

"Oh, stop with all that. I've never met a woman as stubborn as you." Continuing on with hardly a moment's silence, Lynette said, "I can't believe you're getting all freaky about your good luck! And that's what I'm talking about, too. You did get lucky with Ty Slattery."

Oh, Claire hated that perception—that she was so lucky to have gotten a doctor. As if there was nothing more to them than their occupations. Of course, rumors were really going to run rampant when everyone found out she was pregnant. Then people would have no issues about speculating just how she'd managed to "get" Ty.

"I don't want to make a big deal about things yet. I can't believe you told so many people."

"I can't believe you're managing to make a pair of really good events seem like the worst problems ever. You're getting married and having a baby! You get to start over, the second time around, when you're still young enough to enjoy every blessed minute of it!"

"I know."

"Then smile! Your frown ain't no way to go through life, you know."

"Thanks for the support." Claire didn't mean to sound out of sorts, but she felt that way. Lynette was one of the few people who knew just what her circumstances were before arriving at the hospital.

Because of that, Claire would have thought that she'd be more understanding about what a big step it was to jump into another relationship.

The intercom buzzed. "Claire or Lynette, could one of you help us out in emergency for an hour?" the office manager in charge called out. "It's busy today and Joan needs to go to lunch."

"I'll do it," Claire volunteered before Lynette could say a word. She needed a change of scenery and a break in their conversation. And, well, in the emergency room, she'd have a better chance to see Ty.

"I'm still going to plan something," Lynette said in parting. "A big party or shower. You're going to enjoy it, too."

"Thank you."

Lynette kept talking like Claire hadn't said a word. "Yes, indeed. Something with balloons and streamers. And a cake. Something big and flashy and involving a buffet."

For the next hour, Claire didn't have time to think about anything but what was going on right in front of her. The emergency room was nuts. She just concentrated on doing her job, stopping only to ask questions about where to direct people.

In the middle of the chaos, Deanna Johns came in carrying her little girl, Annie. Though Deanna did look a little more rested, she was still wearing dark circles under her eyes.

To another receptionist, Claire said, "I'll help her. She came in a month ago." Thinking quickly, she asked, "Hey, is Dr. Slattery here?"

A knowing glance turned her way. "Missing him already, Claire?"

Though she felt a blush coming on, Claire fought against the wave of embarrassment. "He helped her son the last time she was here. I thought a familiar face might be a good thing."

Comprehension dawned. "I'll check."

Meanwhile, at the door, Deanna paused to shift her daughter before stepping forward.

Claire pointed to her cubicle. "Hi, Ms. Johns, do you remember me? I'm Claire Grant, I escorted you to emergency about a month ago."

"I do." A wan smile replaced the lines of worry. "You told me about Applewood."

Claire couldn't have been more gratified. "Did you call?"

"I did one better than that. I met the director and she found us a room. We're now officially off the streets."

"That's wonderful."

"It's *miraculous*, that's what it is. Just a few weeks ago, I didn't know if our luck was ever going to change. I'm in the process of trying to find a job now. I'll be on my way if we can get this little thing fixed up." Meeting Claire's eyes, all the worry that had only been peeking near the surface rose unmistakably. "Annie's fever was 104 degrees when I left."

"Let's get your paperwork started. I asked someone to find Dr. Slattery, too. We'll get Annie seen as soon as possible."

An orderly approached. "Dr. Slattery said to come on back, Claire."

"Thank you. I'll walk her in. Let's go, Ms. Johns." Her pulse did a jump as she walked beside Deanna. Claire did her best to ignore the sensation. She was just worried about Annie. It had nothing to do with seeing Ty.

But it did.

When they met, he was just as calm and competent as ever, immediately putting the little girl at ease. "Annie, you came back to see me?"

A tiny smile appeared and with it Deanna seemed more relaxed. "You think you can figure out what's wrong with her?"

"I'll do my best."

Then to Claire's amusement and happiness, he caught her eye for a split second and shared a smile. "Thanks for bringing Deanna and Annie over."

A simple smile, meaning the world. Making her want to celebrate her new happiness with balloons and cake and one of Lynette's buffets.

What had happened to her?

NINE WEEKS. She was nine weeks pregnant. She'd given in and checked out some pregnancy books from the library and had taken to reading them—and dreaming about holding a new little one—every night before bedtime.

Her body was still only really enjoying soda crackers

and Sprite, but the overwhelming nausea had subsided. Her formerly flat abdomen was now slightly rounded.

Her baby was on the way.

And in spite of herself, she'd begun to plan.

So had Wes. Gradually, he was warming up to the idea of all the dramatic changes that were about to take place. He peppered her with a lot of questions during odd times.

"Which room at Ty's am I going to get?"

"I don't know. Maybe the guest bedroom?"

"It's got gray walls. I'm going to want blue. Or red. Can I paint my walls?"

"Definitely not red. We'll talk to Ty about blue. Remember, though, it's not Ty's house. He's a renter."

"His place is better."

She'd give him that. "We'll like the space."

"And Maisy."

"And Maisy."

"Do you think Maisy will like the baby?"

"I hope so."

"Do you feel different 'cause you're pregnant?"

"Sometimes."

"Can you feel the baby?"

"Not usually."

"When are you going to tell everyone?"

"When I'm three months. That's the usual time."

"Then we'll get married."

"Then we'll move in. We're going to wait to get married, Wes. I told you that. Now, eat your burger."

WHILE THEY WERE COOKING dinner with Ty a week later, everything turned on its side again.

"Claire, something happened today I want to talk to you about," Ty said as he pulled out a head of lettuce from the fridge and started rinsing it off.

"What's that?"

"I was offered a job in Chicago." Turning off the sink faucet, he said, "It's a good job. Lots of opportunity, with a big practice. They talked money. The money's really good, Claire."

She stopped slicing mushrooms and looked at him for the first time. Tried to take herself out of the picture, but it was hard because, well, she *was* in the picture. "And?"

"It's a good opportunity." He paused for a moment. "Actually, I'm going to go up there this weekend and check things out."

He was going. To check things out. Each word felt like a lead stone in her stomach. "But, what about Wes and me?"

"I'll miss you both, but it's only for the night."

He didn't get it. "I'm not talking about the trip, I'm talking about the decision."

"No decision's been made yet. Only an offer. A really good offer."

"But Ty, don't you think you should have talked about this with me?"

"We're talking now." With sure hands, he began ripping the lettuce into bite-size pieces.

"I feel like you're already on the verge of accepting it. And you and I will need to think things through before you do that."

"There's really nothing to talk about," he said slowly. Too slowly, in Claire's opinion. He was acting like she couldn't understand him! "I have to get a job."

"But in Chicago? Why aren't you looking around here, in Cincinnati?"

"Nothing's come available around here. I need to go to where the offer is. You've got to know that."

She'd never thought about it, not really. "I didn't think you'd have to take a job so far away."

"Chicago's not that far. It's a good thing, Claire. Surely you didn't think that I'd get hired on at Lane's End Memorial?"

Claire didn't appreciate his attitude. "To be honest, I haven't been thinking about your future job prospects." Curving her arms over her stomach, she added, "I've had other things to think about."

"I've been worrying about things, too. Now I'm going to have you, Wes and a baby. That's a lot of responsibility."

She knew he didn't mean things the way they sounded. Knew he wasn't trying to make her feel bad about getting pregnant. But she did. Instead of rehashing things, she said, "When do you leave?"

"Tomorrow morning."

"All right." Picking up the knife, she went back to work, chopping vegetables, but her enthusiasm for dinner was gone.

Lately, all she'd been thinking about was how hard their changes were going to be—not about how excited she was to begin again. Something was very wrong with that.

Chapter Twenty

"Another Saturday, another wrestling meet," Jill Young said when Claire climbed up the rickety wooden bleachers to join her.

"You said it. This one was hard to get to, though. I didn't know if I was ever going to get here."

Overnight, the unseasonably nice weather had turned and sleet had started to fall. Her little Corolla hadn't taken kindly to the slippery roads. Claire had held the steering wheel in a death grip the last twenty minutes and managed to get there forty minutes late.

Taking her seat, she said, "Has Wes wrestled yet?"

Jill smiled in sympathy. "You just missed him. He won."

Well, of course he won a match when she wasn't there. "What about Mark?"

"He's hanging in there. He won his first match but lost the second."

"You can't win them all."

"That's a fact," Jill said. Rubbing her rear end, she quipped, "The only thing we can depend on is having sore butts when it's all over. These bleachers are a killer."

Claire chuckled as she settled in.

Two hours went by. Outside, the sleet turned to snow. Eventually, they stopped the meet early because of bad weather.

"Be careful out there, parents," Coach Davidson said as they all stood up to go. "We'll see you at school."

Claire dreaded the drive home. She wished she knew some of the other parents well enough to catch a ride. But no one else seemed to be worried about driving, so she supposed she shouldn't be, either.

She found consolation in Wes catching the bus and going to a sleepover with a few boys on the team. She just had to get home then she could put her feet up for the rest of the night.

"Call me in the morning," she told Wes right before leaving. Because there was no way he'd accept a hug or a kiss, Claire settled for a pat on the shoulder before heading back outside and scraping off her windshield.

Traffic was thick and cars were moving slowly on the highway. Carefully she merged, then merged again, this time onto I-71, staying in the slow lane and taking her time.

But she hardly had time to do more than gasp when the black pickup in front of her fishtailed, then slid into her lane. Around her, all other cars braked hard to get out of the way. She did the same. Her Corolla skipped, skidded, then lost its fight with the treacherous road and careened to the right. Claire did her best to regain control, but it was a lost cause.

In a series of subsequent moves and jerks, her car smashed into the pickup, then into the guardrail. Finally it crashed to a stop when the car from behind slammed into her.

As the seat belt gripped her hard while the rest of her body met the force of the collision, Claire knew she was in trouble. Pain shot through her arm as she attempted to shield her face from glass. And as her abdomen burned and she fought to retain consciousness, Claire said a little prayer of thanks that Wes wasn't with her. She would die if anything were to happen to him.

Because she was fairly sure she'd just lost her baby.

"Ty!"

"Hey, buddy," Ty said, "I'm glad you called, but I can't talk now, I'm in a series of meetings."

"It's Mom."

Finally, the panic in Wes's voice registered. "What happened?"

"She's been in an accident," he said through tears. "I saw it happen from the bus."

"Whoa. Accident? Bus? What—"

"Hey, doc?" Coach Davidson took over the phone. "On the way home, Claire was involved in a pretty serious accident. Four cars were involved. We were driving by in the bus and saw it."

"How's Claire?" he asked with dread.

"I'm not sure. We couldn't stop, obviously, but ambulances were already on their way. Once we saw Claire was involved, we called the hospital, police and now you." He paused. "Wes said you all have become close?"

"Yes. We're all getting married."

Gene lowered his voice. "Wes whispered something about a baby?"

Ty's heart felt like it was permanently lodged in his

windpipe. "Yes. We weren't broadcasting the news, but Claire's pregnant."

"We'll all be praying for you, Ty."

"Thanks. I…I mean that." Ty had never felt more helpless. Damn. He was five hours away by car on a good day. If the weather was as bad as Gene said, he was going to have a hell of a time getting back. After saying as much to Gene, he said, "Put Wes back on, would you?"

"Ty, where are you?" Wes asked.

"I'm still in Chicago." With supreme effort, he tried to keep his voice positive. "Listen, I'm going to get there as fast as I can. I'm going to see how the airports are. If planes are too delayed, I'll start driving home."

"I'm worried."

Ty clutched the phone a little tighter. "I know you are. But your mom's a fighter, right?"

"Right."

"Coach said he'd take you to the hospital. Call me when you know something, please? I'll call, too."

"Okay."

With shaking hands, Ty hung up, realizing that in the space of five minutes, his whole reality had shifted. Though he'd always valued Claire, now he knew for certain that nothing was more important than being with her and raising their child—their children—together.

"You okay, Dr. Slattery?" Wendy, the office assistant who'd been showing him around the hospital asked.

Ty struggled to find his composure. "My fiancée's been in an accident. I need to get back now."

"Of course you do." Picking up the phone, she said, "Would you like to check flights first?"

"Yeah. Thanks." He was shaking so badly, he sat down while Wendy spoke with an airline representative after a long wait. "Nothing's flying out on time, doctor. Delays could take hours. What do you want to do?"

"I'll start driving. Thanks." He quickly left his business card with his personal information, then practically ran to the parking garage.

"Ty!" Clark, the hospital administrator who'd interviewed him, called out. "Wendy just told me what happened. Wait a minute."

Impatiently, Ty did as he asked, but he really had no desire to do anything but get in his car and go. But to his surprise, Clark appeared five minutes later with a blanket, a paper sack, and a stainless steel carafe. "What's all this?"

"Wendy called over to the cafeteria after she spoke with me. You're going to need some sustenance if you're about to make that drive. Coffee, sandwiches and a blanket, just in case."

"Thanks. I don't know what to say."

Clark laughed. "Come on, you know the answer to that. Thank you."

"Thanks," Ty said, meaning it as he shook Clark's hand.

"Let me know what happens, will you? I know we just met, but we care."

Ty knew Clark did—his actions spoke for themselves. "I will call. Please tell Wendy thanks as well."

"Will do."

TY HAD GONE FORTY MILES when his cell phone rang. Quickly glancing at the phone, he recognized Wes's number. "Wes?"

"No, it's Gene, Ty."

Focus, he thought to himself. Take deep breaths and don't expect the worst. "How's Claire?"

"Not too good." Gene paused. "Ty, I don't know how to tell you this—fact is, I don't even know if I should be telling you this on the road, but I think you're going to need to know before you see Wes or Claire. Ty…Claire lost the baby."

"Oh, God." Purposefully focusing on the road, Ty kept in control. "How's she doing?" Even to his own ears, his voice sounded squeaky. Hoarse.

"Claire's okay. Well, she's okay, all things considered. She's got a broken arm, two cracked ribs and some cuts all over her face and hands, but she's stable. She's pretty drugged up right now, though."

"And Wes?"

Gene paused. "Not so good."

"Can you put him on?"

"I can't right this minute. A bunch of his buddies are here from the team. They took him down to the cafeteria to get something to eat. I thought it might do him good to do that instead of keeping vigil by the door."

"Thanks. And, thank everyone there for me, would you? It means a lot that you're taking care of them both."

"We'll get through it, don't you worry." Gene cleared his throat. "You going to be okay? I guess it's a little late for me to ask but—"

"I'm okay. The roads aren't too bad here, and the traffic is next to nothing."

"Take your time. Like I said, she's sleeping and Wes is in good hands."

"Thanks, Gene. And thanks for telling me…for telling

me about the ba—" he struggled to keep his voice even and steady "—thanks for telling me about the baby."

"I'm sorry as hell about it."

"Me, too. Gene, tell Wes he can call me as soon as he wants."

"I will."

As he clicked off, Ty forced himself to only concentrate on the road. To not think about anything but the highway. There'd be time enough to think about everything else when he spoke to Wes.

When he saw Claire.

Thinking of her smile, her love for Wes, her shy excitement about the baby, he wondered if he'd just lost it all. Would she want to marry him now?

Funny, but now he wanted her in his life more than ever. Thinking about losing Claire and Wes was almost impossible to contemplate.

And yet, as he drove down the highway, it was all he could think about.

Chapter Twenty-One

Seven hours later, Ty strode through the double doors of Lane's End Memorial Hospital with only one thing on his mind—to find Claire as soon as possible. The trip from Chicago had been endless—traffic snarled in Indianapolis and was sluggish all the way going east on I-74 into Cincinnati. Lynette was a welcome sight at the reception counter.

She raced around the horseshoe desk to greet him. "I'm glad you made it safe and sound. I've been worried about something happening to you, too. That's a bear of a drive in weather like this."

It had been the longest of his life. "Thanks for worrying. The Interstate was tough, but that's nothing new. How's Claire? Have you heard anything? The traffic was too bad to keep calling for reports."

"I know she's out of ICU and has been moved to a private room." She smiled slightly. "One of the benefits of working here. Everyone's doing their best to make Claire comfortable."

"Yeah, we do take care of our own, don't we?"

"We take care of everybody. But, yeah, at least we know

if we're in a tough situation, friends are going to come out of the woodwork to help make things all right."

Before Ty could comment on that, Lynette said quietly, "She's in room 322."

"And Wes?"

Her expression softened and, for the first time, she looked like tears were about to flow. "He's there, too. He's been waiting for you and for Claire's friend Tessa. Tessa sent word she'd be here just as soon as she could."

"I'm glad he called her. If anyone asks, that's where I'll be."

"Will do. Let me know if you need anything," she said, walking back to the desk to meet a new arrival.

Ty grabbed the first elevator he could to the third floor, then began the long walk down the hall. Although he'd done this walk more times than he could count, it felt completely different now that the situation was personal.

He nodded to several other doctors and nurses. More than one looked at him in a concerned way, making Ty realize that though he and Claire had done their best to keep things low-key, they hadn't fooled anyone. Everyone knew they were a couple and now knew that they'd been expecting a baby, and had lost it.

Ty couldn't care less what people thought, about their age differences, about their job differences, about their reasons for getting married.

Outside Claire's room, Wes sat by himself. Though every instinct was screaming to go to Claire, a much gentler force instructed him to sit by the boy's side. This boy was hurting. "Hey, buddy," he said.

Wes looked up, a flash of relief so vivid in his eyes that

Ty suddenly felt ten feet tall. He sat down next to him. And then, because it felt right—because it felt like the only thing that really needed to be done—he opened his arms to Wes.

The boy, so scrappy in the wrestling room, so tough and cool around his mom, hiccupped, then launched himself against Ty's chest and began to cry.

Tears pricked Ty's own eyes as he, too, finally let down his guard and allowed himself to feel. Clutching Wes to him more tightly, he buried his face in Wes's narrow shoulder. "She's going to be okay," he murmured. "I know it."

"She looks bad."

"She'll get better soon. The doctors here are the best."

"I feel bad because I was on the bus. I should've been riding with her."

"I feel guilty, too. I was in Chicago. But, we can't take the blame for accidents, right? Sometimes things happen. There's no one to blame."

After another ragged series of tears, Wes wiped his eyes with the bottom of his shirt and pulled away. Ty watched him carefully. "Feel better?"

"Almost." He wiped at his face again. Sounding a little bit more like his usual self, Wes declared, "Being here stinks. It sucks. I hate hospitals."

"I know you do." Stories that Claire had relayed about Wes having to visit her in the hospital years ago came rushing back. Because he didn't want to tiptoe around what had to be very real, concerned feelings, he said, "Bring back memories?"

"It brings back everything." He wrinkled his nose. "I hate the smell here. It smells like sick people."

"It smells like antiseptic."

With a glare toward the nurses' station, he muttered, "I hate it."

Ty winked at the nurse who looked their way in alarm. Tammy had been by his side for more examinations than he could count. She was also experienced enough to not take Wes's glare personally. She held up her mug of coffee, silently offering him a cup.

He shook his head. A hot cup did sound like heaven, but there were other things to do first.

Ty gestured to the closed door to the right of Wes. "I'm about to go on in. Is anyone in there now?"

"I don't think so. All the doctors and nurses were there. I got to go in for a little bit." He gestured toward Tammy again. "But then she made me leave."

"I bet Tammy thought your mom needed her rest."

"I guess." Voice cracking, he added, "Mom looks really bad, Ty. She's got cuts all over her and bruises and tubes."

"When you saw her, was she awake?" Ty hoped there would be something positive they could focus on instead of everything that was wrong. It was a trick he'd taught himself back when his parents divorced and it worked well when dealing with patients.

Wes shrugged. "Kind of."

"Did she recognize you?"

"She smiled and said my name."

"I'd say she did, then." Brushing a thick lock of hair off Wes's forehead, he added, "That's a good thing."

"It means she's going to be okay?"

"I think so. It also means that you're the most important thing in the world to her, right?"

"She's the same way for me," he replied, his voice not quite so reedy. "It's been just the two of us for so long."

"I know."

As if he was taking a huge load off his shoulders, Wes added, "She lost the baby."

"I heard." The pain was still there, practically blinding him with the force of his loss. Surprising him with how much he cared about a baby he'd never intended to have.

Focus on the positive. Focus on what was necessary. "I'm sorry about that." Closing his eyes, Ty cursed himself. He sounded like a jerk. Why couldn't he think of anything more meaningful, more sympathetic to say?

Because it hurt too much.

But if Wes noticed his words were less than perfect, he didn't let on. "Me, too." After a moment, he said, "Do you think she's going to be okay?"

"If she has you and me, she's going to be fine. It just might be a while."

Down the hall, two people approached, a tall guy, solidly built with a swagger that practically screamed cop, and a petite, pretty brunette. The moment they saw Wes, the woman walked forward. "Oh, Wes!"

Like someone had just pressed start, Wes jumped up and wrapped his arms around the woman and held on tight.

"Keaton Phillips," the guy said after patting Wes's back. "My wife Tessa and I are friends of Claire's and Wes's."

"Ty Slattery. Thanks for coming."

Tessa looked up from over Wes's shoulder and gave a quick smile before focusing on Wes again. He was talking a mile a minute, telling Tessa everything.

"I'm glad you two came. Wes called you?" Ty asked.

"Wes called Tessa. I got the news from a cop who was at the accident. He recognized the name. How's Claire doing?"

"I don't know too much. I was just about to go in to see her." Ty paused, unsure of what to say, of what to do. They were engaged. She'd been going to have his baby. But suddenly, it felt like he was the outsider. Like he didn't have as much right to be there as everyone else.

It was damned awkward.

If Keaton sensed that, he didn't let on. Instead he said, "You go in, we'll stay here and chat with Wes."

Ty still wasn't sure what to do. "You okay with that, bud?"

"I'm good," Wes said as Tessa handed him some kind of snack out of her tote bag and started pulling out spare change.

Without another word, Ty opened the door and stepped in.

SURE ENOUGH, Claire was pretty much like Wes had described. Bandaged, bruised and had way too many tubes and cords attached to her. And though Ty knew he should be immune to the machines, everything seemed magnified.

He hated to see the woman he loved hurting.

Though he saw her chart at the end of the bed, Ty ignored it, wanting to touch her instead. Needing the contact. Sinking into the chair next to her, he very carefully caressed her arm. "Oh, Claire."

Moments later her eyelids fluttered open. "Ty. You're here."

"I'm sorry I didn't get here earlier. The weather was horrible. I tried. I promise I tried."

"S'okay."

To his amazement, she reached out for him. Tenderly, he took her hand, careful not to nudge her IV. Careful not to touch any of the cuts or abrasions she'd sustained on her hands and arms.

Thinking of how much worse things could've been, he felt his eyes tear up. With an iron will, he fought them back. The last thing anyone needed was for him to fall apart.

"I—I saw Wes. He's outside talking to Tessa and Keaton."

Relief filled her gaze. "I'm glad they're here."

"I know."

Her eyes drifted shut. Then, with supreme effort, she added, "Ask Tessa if he can stay with them, would you? They're used to him."

He was used to Wes, too. "He doesn't have to go with them. I…can take him home with me." After all, hadn't Wes been about to move into his house anyway?

"Wes loves them. He stays with them a lot."

"Oh. All right."

Her eyes closed, then opened again, searching his face. Ty knew she was waiting for him to say something, to indicate that he knew about the baby. So she wouldn't have to break the news.

Reluctantly, he gave her what she wanted. "I know about the baby, Claire. I'm so sorry, honey."

Her bottom lip trembled. "The doctor said the impact was just too much."

"I'm sorry," he said again. Feeling completely useless. Completely ineffectual. He'd comforted other patients before. Didn't he have anything better to offer?

She shifted, wincing with the effort. Ty attempted to adjust the pillows behind her head.

"The pregnancy never seemed real until this accident," she murmured. "How strange is that?"

"I feel the same way. I was excited, but I felt like it was something someone else was going through." He kissed her knuckles. "But I'm disappointed. I'm going to miss our baby."

Her lip trembled. When a single tear appeared, Ty gently wiped it away. "I'm worried about you, too, honey."

"I'm okay."

Only Claire could say that. Attempting to lighten things up, to calm her down, he said, "Not too okay. You've looked better."

A quick, sudden laugh escaped and her eyes widened in surprise. "I hope I've looked better. I hurt all over," she admitted. "I feel like I've been hit by a truck."

He couldn't help but smile, too. "Bad joke."

"I know."

Her eyelids drooped. Exhaustion had settled in. "Why don't you rest now?"

"You leaving?"

"No. I'm not leaving. I'll be right here when you wake up."

"Promise?"

"I promise," he said, realizing it was the easiest promise he'd ever made.

After watching her for a while and seeing that she was in a deep sleep, Ty stepped out. Tessa, Keaton and Wes were all sipping hot chocolate. Three pairs of eyes met his. "She's sleeping."

"That's good, right?" Tessa asked.

"Yep. Sleep is the best thing for her." Pointing to their cups, he said, "How is it?"

"Not as bad as you might think," Keaton said. "Want one?"

"No, thanks." Remembering what he and Claire had

talked about, Ty ventured, "Wes, your mom is sleeping now, but I did talk to her for a bit. She said if you wanted, you could either stay with me or with Keaton and Tessa." Remembering his manners, he apologized. "Sorry, I didn't even ask if you were able to have him over."

"We always want him over," Tessa said. "What do you think, bud? Want to come home with us for a day or two?"

To Ty's surprise, Wes turned to him. "Mom said I could stay with you?"

"Of course," he lied, but not feeling bad about it. Ty had a feeling that Claire had just assumed he wouldn't want to take care of Wes. But he did. Part of him really wanted that boy around. Wanted his company. "I'd love to have you stay at my place, if you want to."

"I'd rather do that."

He felt completely humbled. "Good. Maisy will be thrilled."

Wes turned to Tessa and Keaton, who were holding hands. "Do you mind?"

"Not at all. In fact, I think that's a great idea," Tessa said, surprising Ty. "This way you can be near your mom with Ty here in Lane's End."

Too emotional to speak, Ty nodded his thanks. Keaton nodded back before speaking. "Since your mom's sleeping right now, maybe we could get something to eat."

"Pizza sounds good," Tessa said.

Wes perked up. "Pepperoni?"

"Is there any other kind?"

Wes stood up. "I am kind of hungry."

Tessa laughed as she stood up, too. "How about we bring you back a pizza, Ty?"

He wasn't hungry, but because he knew what it was like to want to help, even if it was just bringing food, he thanked them. Then, after arranging for them to bring Wes back in two hours, the three of them left, leaving Ty alone again.

Tammy brought him a mug of coffee. "I just made it, so it's actually pretty decent."

He took a sip. Hot and with a healthy dose of real milk, it definitely hit the spot. "Thanks. It's good."

She patted his shoulder in a motherly way. "You going to be okay, doc?"

"Me? I'm fine."

He walked back to Claire's side and reached for her hand again. She opened one eye, almost smiled, then went back to sleep.

For the first time since they'd found out about her pregnancy, Ty felt as if he'd finally become part of the family.

Yes, he was crushed about the baby and worried sick about Claire. But he was also extremely gratified to know that nothing mattered but the future they were going to have together.

The three of them.

IT WAS AFTER MIDNIGHT when he and Wes got back to his place. Wes had fallen asleep in the car on the way home. "Let's get inside and we'll get you ready for bed," Ty said as he guided Wes out of the cold and into the house.

"I don't have any of my stuff."

"I have an extra toothbrush and you can borrow a shirt or something of mine to sleep in, okay?"

"Okay." Wes slipped off his tennis shoes and followed Ty into the living room.

Maisy came over to greet them. Because he knew she wouldn't go far so late in the middle of the night, Ty just let her out while he got Wes settled.

In no time, Wes was ready for bed. Maisy had indeed come back, and seemed to be doing her best to make the boy feel welcome.

Both she and Ty followed Wes to the guest bedroom. With a yawn, Wes climbed into the turned-down sheets. "This was going to be my room."

Was? "You mean when your mom and I get married?"

Sad, somber eyes stared back. "Yeah."

"Why do you act like it won't be now?"

"'Cause you and Mom aren't going to have a baby anymore."

Helplessly, Ty sank to his side. "Wes, we didn't want to get married just because of the baby. I still want to marry your mom. I still want you to live here, too."

Wes looked skeptical. "But there's no reason any longer."

"I'd say there's more of a reason now than ever. We're all going to need each other. That's what people do in tough times, you know?"

Looking far older than thirteen, Wes said, "My dad left us."

"I know he did. But I'm not like him. I don't leave and I don't want us to end."

"I don't want us to end, either."

"Good." Swallowing the lump in his throat, Ty said, "You mean a lot to me. Even if I didn't love your mom, you'd still mean a lot to me."

Wes didn't reply because his eyes had already drifted closed. Maisy whined, so Ty let her jump onto the mattress next to the boy, to keep him warm and give him comfort.

And then he quietly left, went to the kitchen and pulled out a beer.

In his dark living room, he sat, thinking about the tour of the hospital, the long drive, the hours next to Claire. The tough conversations he'd had with other staff members.

Finally, the talk he'd just had with Wes. Tragedies showed just how much people cared. Just how much they meant to each other. And no doubt about it, Claire and Wes meant everything to him.

He sipped his beer, then finally rested his head against the back cushion of the couch and closed his eyes.

Enjoying the quiet of the moment for the first time all day.

Chapter Twenty-Two

"I don't need a wheelchair," Claire protested, feeling grumpy from the pain, from her circumstances, from being without a car. She felt grumpy with pretty much the whole world.

"Doctor's orders. You don't leave the hospital unless you're in a wheelchair," Lynette said. "I would have thought you would've remembered that."

The last thing she needed was to be reminded about rules and regulations. "I'm going to be fine. All I need to do is—"

"You broke your arm. You've got more cuts and scrapes on you than an entire pro football team." One of Lynette's hips jutted out, a sure sign she was done being talked down to. "I know you don't need me to give you a rundown of your injuries—you've got to be feeling them just fine. Lord, girl. Settle down and give me a break. Don't be so fussy."

"Give you a break? Don't be fussy?" In the past Claire had always appreciated Lynette's no-nonsense Southern attitude. Now that she was on the receiving end, she had to admit the ordering just made her feel even more out of sorts. "Lynette, you don't need to tell me again what's wrong."

"Then let me do my job, will you, please?"

The fight went out of her. "Sorry. I'll settle down."

"About time."

"I am the patient here, you know. You're supposed to be nice to me."

"I was nice to you. Two days ago."

Lynette had been more than nice; she'd been positively angelic. She'd visited Claire several times a day, helped with Wes when Ty couldn't and had just clasped her hand when Claire burst into tears when she felt the loss of the baby was more than she could bear.

Lynette had even snuck in a piece of coconut cream pie when Claire admitted she couldn't take any more Jell-O and soup. Now she was wheeling Claire out while Ty pulled up his vehicle. "You've been a great friend." Looking up behind her, she caught Lynette's eye. "Have I thanked you enough?"

"You've thanked me," Lynette said gruffly. "No need to say it again."

"I don't know what I would have done without you."

"You'd have done the same for me. And have, on occasion. Remember when my washing machine flooded and I stayed with you for a week?"

"That was nothing."

"That was something. Don't knock it. Now hush for a second, would you?" Lynette turned on her professional charm and slowly guided Claire through the halls and backed her into the elevator.

When the doors opened, Lynette made a sharp right turn and picked up the pace. "Ah, look who's here. Our handsome resident, Dr. Slattery."

He trotted up to meet them, taking over control of the wheelchair's handles. "How's she doing?"

"Must be better because she's complaining at every turn."

Claire tilted her head back. "I am not complaining!"

"See what I mean?"

Ty chuckled. "Don't worry, honey. I'd be complaining, too."

"I haven't been complaining," she said, then stopped when she saw the look of amusement pass between Ty and Lynette. Finally, she got it. They'd been having a good time teasing her. "Okay, maybe a little."

Outside, the weather was frosty, but not unbearable. Ty noticed her shiver. "We'll get you warm soon." Next he opened his Jeep's door, helped Claire slide in, carefully buckled her seat belt, then kissed her brow. "Ready?"

"Almost." Turning to Lynette, she said, "You'll come by in a few days?"

"I'm bringing dinner on Wednesday."

To her amazement, staff had gotten together and made a schedule to provide her with meals. In between, parents from the wrestling team had volunteered to help out, too. At first Claire had wanted to refuse such generosity, but Ty had pushed her protests away. "This is going to be the best I've ever eaten in my life. Let them do it…Wes will like the food, too."

So in the end, she'd ended up saying thank you. She was getting pretty good at saying that.

THE WEATHER HAD HELD OFF for the last week, even going so far as to warm up to an almost balmy forty-eight degrees. The unexpected warmth had melted the last of the snow and dried the streets.

It was the time of the year she liked the least. Thanksgiving and Christmas were just memories and the pleasure of nesting inside during cold winter days had long since come and gone. It was too soon to start looking for crocuses or buds on trees. Most days, the skies were cloudy. And though she'd tried hard to lift her spirits, she felt depressed and in between things.

"You okay?" Ty asked.

"I'm fine."

"As soon as we get home, I'll get you settled in bed."

His bed. Were they even still engaged, now that there was no reason to rush things? The hospital hadn't been the place to discuss their future but something needed to be said, soon.

A void had opened between them, as empty and nasty as their warm, hopeful conversations had been about babies and baby names. Ty hadn't said much about the miscarriage. Instead, he'd focused on her other injuries, obviously having an easier time talking about them than of the hurt losing the baby had caused.

But now, as he drove down Mission Street, Claire felt the void that had developed between them was in danger of swallowing her up. They were going to need to discuss things. Soon. There was no choice. They needed to sort things out before they rushed back into a future that maybe he didn't even really want.

They needed to have this discussion before she started thinking of his place as home. Before Wes started thinking of Ty as his dad. Before she started depending on him.

But was it already too late?

Ty parked in the one-car garage. Claire waited for him to help her out, then, with his support, slowly walked into the house.

Just as he crossed the living room, walking toward his bedroom, Claire knew that suddenly being in his bed surrounded by all things Ty was going to be too much. It was going to be bad enough having to rely on him, she definitely did not need to be surrounded by his scent 24-7 while she was recovering.

"Would you mind if I took over the couch instead?"

He glanced at her. "Sure. The…couch is fine."

They got her settled. She was more tired from the trip to Ty's than she'd expected. However, it was time to talk about their future. She'd never be able to relax if she didn't say what needed to be said as soon as possible. "When do you go in for work?"

"Not for three days. I asked for some time off."

"Is that allowed?"

"I guess it will have to be. Besides, my last rotation is pretty much done. Most everyone is interviewing now, anyway. Don't worry, Claire, everyone understands that we need to be together."

That was the problem. It felt like everyone did…but her. "Can we talk?"

"Now?"

"Well, yeah."

He pulled up the ottoman and rested his elbows on his knees. "Anything in particular?"

"Us." Taking a deep breath, she said, "So, you know… we don't have to get married anymore."

His face turned expressionless. "Because there's no baby?"

Oh, that hurt! "Yes. Because of that."

He swallowed. "I thought we had something between us, Claire. You know, I've been taking care of Wes."

"You've been great. And, I appreciate everything you've done for me. But we don't have to rush into things now."

"Claire, when I heard about your accident, I thought a part of me was going to break into pieces."

"Because of the baby."

"Yes. And no, dammit. I was worried about you, too. Don't you get it? I love you."

Shaken, Claire fought to remain strong. "I love you, too."

"Then what's the problem? We love each other. I love your kid, I want to be together."

"Ty, that might not be enough."

Pure frustration filled his gaze. "What more do you need?"

"Stability. We've still got a lot of obstacles in between us."

"Such as?"

"You owe a fortune."

"Claire, I wish you wouldn't talk like I lost everything gambling or on some crazy shopping spree."

"It doesn't change the fact that a bank is expecting you to pay them back."

His expression hardened. "It changes everything. Honestly, Claire, the bank trusts me, why can't you?"

Because she'd done that before. She'd put her blind faith in a man and he'd betrayed her many times over.

"There's nothing I can do about that except promise you that I'll pay off my loans as quickly as I'm able."

"But what if something happens to you? If we're married, I'll have to pay them and I don't know if I can do that again."

"I'm…not…Ray." Each angry word sounded wrenched

from his soul. As if she'd pushed him and his strength to the limit.

And maybe she had. He certainly wasn't Ray. Ty was as different from Ray as night and day.

But that didn't mean everything between them was perfect. "There's also the differences in our ages," she said. But even to her ears, that excuse sounded lame. Four years wasn't all that much.

Ty stood up and backed away. "I can't do anything about my age, Claire."

"I know." Finally, she played her last card—her last doubt. "Then, there's that job you interviewed for. In Chicago."

"They offered it to me."

She'd known they would. She also knew enough about the medical profession to know that Ty would have been a fool not to take it. But the fact that they hadn't even discussed their future together grated on her.

Just as much as the fact that she was going to have to uproot her son from the first stable environment he'd ever had. "What did you decide to do?"

"I took it."

"I see."

"Claire, I had to take it."

He was making everything happen so fast! So quickly. She was still trying to come to grips that she wasn't about to have a baby within the year. Didn't he understand? She was still mourning their baby. Because saying that wouldn't help, she asked the only thing she could. "When do you have to go?"

"I don't know. Pretty soon. Spring."

That would mean pulling Wes out of school midyear.

So many changes. So amazingly fast. "Can't we just take more time?"

"Is that all you want? Just more time? I'm sorry, but it doesn't feel that way to me. I feel like you don't want to go at all. That you're looking for a way out."

"What do you want me to say, Ty? That I would willingly move Wes, uproot his life again?"

"Don't bring Wes into this. You're not worried about him, you're worried about *you* being uprooted. You're worried about starting over again."

In a burst of clarity, she realized he was right. She was scared, plain and simple. She was scared to trust again, scared to start over again, scared to believe in a man who seemed too good to be true. "Maybe I am," she said slowly.

"Well, at least you're finally being honest." He walked to the small kitchen, poured a glass of orange juice from the fridge and drank it quickly, his back to her. "I think you've already decided you don't want to be with me."

"I haven't done that." Had she?

"It sure seems that way to me," he said facing her once again. "You know, I have doubts, too. My mom took off when I was a whole lot younger than Wes. Sharon left when my future didn't look as rosy as she wanted it to be. I don't know if I believe in happy endings, either, but I'm willing to try."

She'd always thought she'd want to try again, too. Deep sadness filled her. What had happened to hope?

Ty approached again. "It really doesn't matter that I love you and Wes, does it?"

"Of course it matters." It mattered a lot. But…what if

things still fell apart? At one time, she'd been sure she'd loved Ray. She didn't know if she could face another winter homeless. If she could handle Wes having to worry about her living or dying again. And because of that bone-crunching fear, she said nothing.

"I want you to stay here until you can get around better. But then I think it's best if you plan to go on home."

"I can go back today."

"Stop being so stubborn for a few minutes, will you? Then, maybe it's best if we just call things off."

"If that's what you want."

"Claire, don't you see? We could have had everything. I wanted to have everything. You weren't willing to take that risk."

"I've already taken risks. It took me to a homeless shelter."

"No, it gave you Wes. It gave you Tessa and Keaton. It gave you your job here and it gave you me." He shook his head in disgust. "No, things weren't clean and pretty, but they worked out okay."

"I just don't want to do things for all the wrong reasons."

"Claire, that's where *you're* wrong. We could have had it all…for all the right reasons."

He grabbed his cell phone and car keys. "Call me if you need anything. I can't stay here right now."

And from her spot on the couch, Claire watched the man who cared so much walk out of her life.

Well, she sure wasn't a victim, was she? No, she was strong and tough and dumb. Single-handedly, she'd managed to push away the best guy she'd met in her life and break her heart all at the same time.

She should be proud of herself.

Closing her eyes, she tried to fight the tears. But they came anyway. Falling down her cheeks. Reminding her that life was for living, not just getting by.

Chapter Twenty-Three

Two weeks had passed. Finally the gray skies had cleared and the long awaited crocuses and daffodils had sprouted through the damp ground. Spring was on its way.

Wrestling season ended. Wes decided against baseball and was running track instead. Life had moved on.

Claire went back to work. Absently, she began to contemplate a new position at the hospital, one that would require training but would allow her to work one-on-one with patients. For reasons she couldn't name, she was reluctant to follow up on the posting for an X-ray technician and complete the paperwork. It didn't seem the right time to make a change. Claire wasn't sure if it was because of the effects of the miscarriage or her breakup with Ty.

She missed him. She missed looking forward to being with him, missed planning meals together. Missed planning a life together. It didn't help that the whole mess was her fault.

Lynette spent each day sharing her opinions…all of which started and ended with "You're making a big mistake, Claire." Sometimes Claire was pretty sure Lynette was right.

Most of the time she was *very* sure Lynette was right.

But it wouldn't matter soon, anyway. Through the grapevine she'd heard that Ty was scheduled to leave within the next month. Claire supposed that would make things easier. The break would force her to go back to her old way of life. Back to thinking that having no romance in her life was a good thing—then she wouldn't get hurt.

It was really too bad she was hurting a lot now.

"HEY, LOOK WHO decided to stop by for a visit," Lynette said as they noticed Deanna Johns walking on the sidewalk. "If I didn't recognize that auburn hair, I'd think that was someone other than our girl."

Claire had to admit Lynette had a point. Dressed in simple slacks, sweater and with her hair pulled neatly back into a clip, Deanna looked far different from the first time she'd entered Lane's End Memorial. "She looks so pretty."

"She sure does." Lynette hopped down from her chair. "Deanna. Hey, girl."

Sliding a pair of sunglasses on top of her head, Deanna grinned at them both. "Hey right back at ya."

Claire looked toward the sidewalk. "I don't see a kid in sight. Are you on your own today? Gosh, are you sick?"

Eyes sparkling, Deanna shook her head. "Nobody's sick, I'm here to see you, Claire. I was wondering if you could spare me a few minutes."

"Go on," Lynette said. "I've got things covered just fine here."

Claire guided Deanna to a section of chairs in the back. "You look so good. How are you?"

"Better than good. Two weeks ago, after Annie and I

were here, I called up your friend Tessa Phillips. Soon after, I went to Designs for Success."

Claire remembered well her own visit to the shop that helped outfit disadvantaged women with clothes and interview skills. Just trying on the gently worn dresses and suits had made her feel worthy and excited about her future. "How did it go?"

"Great. I spoke with Tessa, we talked about my skills and she helped me pick out a business outfit. I just found out I have a second interview at a child-care center this afternoon." She waved a hand, showing neatly filed fingernails. "Tessa called me this morning and said she heard this interview was just a formality. I think I've got a job, Claire. A good one."

Claire couldn't stop smiling. "This is the best news I've heard all week. Thank you so much for coming in to tell me."

"I had to tell you in person, Miss Grant. You're the reason it's all going so well. When we first met, I was so stuck just trying to get by that I forgot to dream a little. Thanks for reminding me to do that."

Claire held back tears. How had she forgotten, that, too? "You're welcome," she finally said.

Deanna stood up. "I know you've got to get back to work and I've got a hundred things to do. Thanks again."

"Let me know how that job goes."

"I will."

"Deanna has a second job interview today," Claire explained to Lynette as they watched Deanna exit the building. "At a daycare center."

"I guess she decided to take some chances with her life and move on, huh?"

Claire knew exactly what Lynette meant by that not-so-subtle hint. She also knew Lynette was right.

It had taken a visit from Deanna to remind her that it was sometimes a very good thing to step out of a comfort zone and walk into the future.

Especially when that comfort zone wasn't very comfortable.

"Do you mind if I take the rest of my break now?"

"Maybe." Lynette raised an eyebrow. "Are you finally going to see someone you should've seen some time ago?"

"I am."

"Go on, Claire. And don't hurry back."

With a bit of good luck, Claire managed to find Ty just as he was ending his shift. "Hey, Claire."

Unable to help herself, she reached out to him. "Ty, can we talk? Or have I completely messed everything up?"

Very slowly, Ty curved his palm over her hand. "We can talk, if that's what you want. When?"

"Today? Soon?" Now that she'd come to her senses, she didn't want to wait another day before planning a future with Ty. If he'd still have her.

His fingers tightened, showing that he, too, was trying his best to hide some strong emotions. "I'm about to leave for the day. When do you get off?"

"In two hours."

"Want to meet me at the park by my house? We could walk Maisy."

"I'll be there. I promise."

"Good." Their hands separated, but the look in his eyes made her heart beat a little faster.

So did that smile.

It was time to accept the facts—she wasn't going to be happy until she set her sights on the future and believed that good things *could* happen. She needed to give love and marriage another try…even if she was scared.

THEY WENT TO THE PARK. Shoots of early daffodils peeked through fresh mulch. Buds on trees hinted that the air would turn warmer very soon.

In the distance, a few kids played on the green aluminum swing sets, a pile of coats lay on the grass nearby.

By mutual agreement, she and Ty walked along the narrow gravel-covered path around Mallard Pond, though there were no ducks today.

As the kids' laughter rang in the distance, Claire started talking. "So. Something pretty great happened at the hospital today."

"What was that?"

"Deanna Johns stopped by to tell me that she got her life back on track. She actually has a job interview today."

"That's great. Really great."

"I thought so, too." She cleared her throat. "Deanna reminded me about something. About how comfort zones sometimes aren't too comfortable at all. And, well, that's what I've been thinking, too, Ty. I was hoping we could try again."

Instead of the joy she'd hoped would fill those blue eyes, resignation colored them instead. "I'm not sure what that means to you."

Reaching for him, she said, "I changed my mind. I've been thinking about things since I went home. I've been thinking about things for a while, actually. Ty, I finally realized that everything can be okay…if we're together."

"Claire, if you change your mind again—"

She stopped him with a fierce hug. "I won't," she whispered. "I promise I won't."

Miraculously, his arms curved around her, pulling her close. "Thank God."

Burying her face in his neck, she whispered, "I've been so lonely without you. Please forgive me."

"There's nothing to forgive," he said, kissing her cheeks. "I know I pushed you. I know you were scared. I love you so much, but I'm not perfect. I know I made mistakes."

"Don't you know I'm okay with that? I make mistakes, too. Pushing you away was a big one. I love you, too."

Ty pulled her into a hug again. Just feeling his arms around her, feeling his warmth, made everything right. Claire rested her head on his chest and just enjoyed the feeling of being back where she needed to be. Ty kissed her forehead, then, ever so gently, guided her chin up.

She shifted and stood on her tiptoes and kissed him. They'd shared passion. This time when their lips met, it was all about forgiveness and love. Tenderness and commitment.

"Claire Grant, will you marry me?" he said, pulling away from her only slightly.

"Yes," she said simply, as in the background two ducks squawked overhead and children played, as the crisp spring air cooled her cheeks and Ty's warm embrace made everything in the world feel perfect.

They kissed again, then Ty stepped back. "We need to talk to Wes."

"He's at our apartment…another mom brought him home today. Would you like to come over for dinner tonight?"

He pretended to consider. "What are you making?"

"Pot roast."

"That's one of my favorites."

The tenderness in his eyes felt like a gift. So did the way he made her feel. "I know."

"I'll be there in two hours. There's something I need to pick up for Wes."

"I have to tell you, I'm not sure how he's going to react."

"I know. But I have an idea." Walking her back to her car, he said, "Trust me?"

"I do," Claire said with a smile. She completely, totally trusted Ty Slattery. And that, well, was the most incredible feeling in the world.

THEY'D EATEN POT ROAST and mashed potatoes. Ty had brought Maisy with him and she'd stationed herself right next to Wes, who pretended he didn't hand her scraps off his plate.

After the first few minutes, conversation between the three of them was like it used to be. Honest and full of humor and teasing. And as Claire watched both of her guys together, she wondered how she could have been so worried about the three of them having a future together.

Finally, Ty picked up a paper bag. "Wes, would you look at these with me?"

Curious, Wes followed Ty to the couch and sat beside him. Claire followed, sitting in the recliner. She was ready to give them space, but was just as curious as to what was in the bag. From the moment he arrived, Ty hadn't given her a single clue.

Without much fanfare, Ty handed the bag to Wes. He eagerly opened it, then raised an eyebrow when he pulled out the contents. "The *Chicago Area Home Guide?*"

Ty nodded. "Yep. I, uh, went to a big Realtor in town this afternoon and picked these up."

Wes looked from Claire to Ty. "I don't get it."

Before Claire could try to explain, Ty replied. "I asked your mom to marry me today and she said yes."

Wes's eyes widened but, uncharacteristically, he said nothing. Claire's heart sank. *Uh-oh. Was this all a big mistake?*

Ty picked up one of the magazines. Flipping through the pages, he said, "Wes, here's the deal. I love your mom. I've grown to love you, too." Looking up from a page, he met Wes's gaze. "I want us to be a family. A real one."

Claire bit her lip to stifle an onslaught of tears. Just now, there was such hope in her son's eyes, it took her breath away.

Wes was good at not expecting much—at not expecting much from her. He was also good at making do. But now, his expression told a different story. Suddenly, he looked nothing like a teenager with attitude. Now he looked like the boy she'd known and loved from the moment he was born. The boy she'd done everything she could to try to protect and care for.

Ty continued. "Wes, I took a job at a hospital in Chicago. It's a good job. Good enough that we'll be able to afford a house in the suburbs."

Wes pursed his lips together, then gazed at the page Ty had stopped on. Slowly, he asked, "A house like one of these? A house with a yard?"

Ty pointed to one of the black-and-white photographs. Claire leaned over and looked, too.

In truth, it was just a modest ranch, nothing too fancy by anyone's standards. But to Claire, it looked like a castle. Flowers bloomed in mulch-covered beds by the front door. A tall oak tree shaded most of the front yard.

Wes ran his finger over the photo. "Look, Ty. It has a fireplace."

Ty nodded. "Yep. We'd be set if the power went out, wouldn't we?" Leaning closer, he read the blurb under the picture. "Three bedrooms, two baths." He smiled. "So far, it has everything we need. It has a fence, too. Maisy would like this place."

Wes turned to Claire. "If we move to Chicago, we'll all be starting over. All of us, together."

Claire nodded, words doing their best to get stuck in her throat. "You're right." Struggling to keep the emotion from her voice, she said, "When we all get married and move to Chicago, we'll get to start over, fresh."

"With a home," Wes pronounced.

"That's right," she whispered as tears threatened to fall. She thought about everything the two of them had been through. Living with, divorcing, then ultimately losing Ray. Living on the streets, digging in Dumpsters for cans. Rooms in shelters, crummy apartments.

This second chance was a gift that she'd never expected, but that she and Wes had always secretly hoped for. "Finally, we'll be a real family in a home of our very own."

Taking the magazine from Ty, Wes studied the picture again very carefully. Then he turned to Claire. With a smile that shone from his heart, he said exactly what the three of them were feeling. "I'm glad."

She couldn't help but share a smile with Ty. Reaching out to him, she clasped his hand. "I'm glad, too. Very, very glad."

* * * * *

THOROUGHBRED LEGACY
The stakes are high when it comes to love,
horse racing, family secrets
and broken promises.

A new exciting
Harlequin continuity series coming soon!
Led by New York Times *bestselling author*
Elizabeth Bevarly
FLIRTING WITH TROUBLE

Here's a preview!

THE DOOR CLOSED behind them, throwing them into darkness and leaving them utterly alone. And the next thing Daniel knew, he heard himself saying, "Marnie, I'm sorry about the way things turned out in Del Mar."

She said nothing at first, only strode across the room and stared out the window beside him. Although he couldn't see her well in the darkness—he still hadn't switched on a light...but then, neither had she—he imagined her expression was a little preoccupied, a little anxious, a little confused.

Finally, very softly, she said, "Are you?"

He nodded, then, worried she wouldn't be able to see the gesture, added, "Yeah. I am. I should have said good-bye to you."

"Yes, you should have."

Actually, he thought, there were a lot of things he should have done in Del Mar. He'd had *a lot* riding on the Pacific Classic, and even more on his entry, Little Joe, but after meeting Marnie, the Pacific Classic had been the last thing on Daniel's mind. His loss at Del Mar had pretty much ended his career before it had even begun, and he'd had to start all over again, rebuilding from nothing.

He simply had not then and did not now have room in his life for a woman as potent as Marnie Roberts. He was a horseman first and foremost. From the time he was a schoolboy, he'd known what he wanted to do with his life—be the best possible trainer he could be.

He had to make sure Marnie understood—and he understood, too—why things had ended the way they had eight years ago. He just wished he could find the words to do that. Hell, he wished he could find the *thoughts* to do that.

"You made me forget things, Marnie, things that I really needed to remember. And that scared the hell out of me. Little Joe should have won the Classic. He was by far the best horse entered in that race. But I didn't give him the attention he needed and deserved that week, because all I could think about was you. Hell, when I woke up that morning all I wanted to do was lie there and look at you, and then wake you up and make love to you again. If I hadn't left when I did—the way I did—I might still be lying there in that bed with you, thinking about nothing else."

"And would that be so terrible?" she asked.

"Of course not," he told her. "But that wasn't why I was in Del Mar," he repeated. "I was in Del Mar to win a race. That was my job. And my work was the most important thing to me."

She said nothing for a moment, only studied his face in the darkness as if looking for the answer to a very important question. Finally she asked, "And what's the most important thing to you now, Daniel?"

Wasn't the answer to that obvious? "My work," he answered automatically.

She nodded slowly. "Of course," she said softly. "That is, after all, what you do best."

Her comment, too, puzzled him. She made it sound as if being good at what he did was a bad thing.

She bit her lip thoughtfully, her eyes fixed on his, glimmering in the scant moonlight that was filtering through the window. And damned if Daniel didn't find himself wanting to pull her into his arms and kiss her. But as much as it might have felt as if no time had passed since Del Mar, there were eight years between now and then. And eight years was a long time in the best of circumstances. For Daniel and Marnie, it was virtually a lifetime.

So Daniel turned and started for the door, then halted. He couldn't just walk away and leave things as they were, unsettled. He'd done that eight years ago and regretted it.

"It *was* good to see you again, Marnie," he said softly. And since he was being honest, he added, "I hope we see each other again."

She didn't say anything in response, only stood silhouetted against the window with her arms wrapped around her in a way that made him wonder whether she was doing it because she was cold, or if she just needed something—someone—to hold on to. In either case, Daniel understood. There was an emptiness clinging to him that he suspected would be there for a long time.

* * * * *

THOROUGHBRED LEGACY
coming soon wherever books are sold!

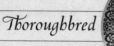 

Cole's Red-Hot Pursuit

Cole Westmoreland is a man who gets what he wants. And he wants independent and sultry Patrina Forman! She resists him—until a Montana blizzard traps them together. For three delicious nights, Cole indulges Patrina with his brand of seduction. When the sun comes out, Cole and Patrina are left to wonder—will this be the end of the passion that storms between them?

Look for

COLE'S RED-HOT PURSUIT

by USA TODAY bestselling author

BRENDA JACKSON

Available in June 2008 wherever you buy books.

Always Powerful, Passionate and Provocative.

REQUEST YOUR FREE BOOKS!

2 FREE NOVELS PLUS 2
FREE GIFTS!

Heart, Home & Happiness!

YES! Please send me 2 FREE Harlequin American Romance® novels and my 2 FREE gifts (gifts are worth about $10). After receiving them, if I don't wish to receive any more books, I can return the shipping statement marked "cancel." If I don't cancel, I will receive 4 brand-new novels every month and be billed just $4.24 per book in the U.S. or $4.99 per book in Canada, plus 25¢ shipping and handling per book and applicable taxes, if any*. That's a savings of close to 15% off the cover price! I understand that accepting the 2 free books and gifts places me under no obligation to buy anything. I can always return a shipment and cancel at any time. Even if I never buy another book from Harlequin, the two free books and gifts are mine to keep forever.

154 HDN EEZK   354 HDN EEZV

Name _____ (PLEASE PRINT) _____

Address _____ Apt. # _____

City _____ State/Prov. _____ Zip/Postal Code _____

Signature (if under 18, a parent or guardian must sign)

Mail to the **Harlequin Reader Service:**
IN U.S.A.: P.O. Box 1867, Buffalo, NY 14240-1867
IN CANADA: P.O. Box 609, Fort Erie, Ontario L2A 5X3

Not valid to current subscribers of Harlequin American Romance books.

Want to try two free books from another line?
Call 1-800-873-8635 or visit www.morefreebooks.com.

* Terms and prices subject to change without notice. N.Y. residents add applicable sales tax. Canadian residents will be charged applicable provincial taxes and GST. This offer is limited to one order per household. All orders subject to approval. Credit or debit balances in a customer's account(s) may be offset by any other outstanding balance`owed by or to the customer. Please allow 4 to 6 weeks for delivery. Offer available while quantities last.

Your Privacy: Harlequin is committed to protecting your privacy. Our Privacy Policy is available online at www.eHarlequin.com or upon request from the Reader Service. From time to time we make our lists of customers available to reputable third parties who may have a product or service of interest to you. If you would prefer we not share your name and address, please check here. ☐

HAR08

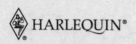
COMING NEXT MONTH

#1213 TEXAS LULLABY by Tina Leonard
The State of Parenthood
Gabriel Morgan has been lured home to Union Junction, Texas, by a father who claims his intentions have nothing to do with matching his ornery son with a ready-made family. Gabriel has his commitment radar up—so when he lays eyes on Laura Adams and her sweet children, he's not prepared for the visions of baby booties dancing in his head!

#1214 MAN OF THE YEAR by Lisa Ruff
From their first meeting, sparks fly between Samantha James and Jarrett Corliss. But Samantha wants nothing to do with the arrogant baseball player. Besides, the team's owner has decreed that there will be no hint of scandal or heads will roll. Jarrett sees Samantha's aloofness as a challenge, and he's not going to let her get away, whatever the boss says.

#1215 AN HONORABLE TEXAN by Victoria Chancellor
Brody's Crossing
Eighteen months ago Cal Crawford left his Texas ranch for deployment overseas, and has returned to find out he's a father. The traditional Cal wants to marry the mother, but Christie Simmons needs to know they are together for love, and not just for the sake of the baby. Can their weekend tryst turn into a lifetime of happiness?

#1216 RELUCTANT PARTNERS by Kara Lennox
Second Sons
When Cooper Remington arrives in Port Clara, Texas, to collect his inheritance, he finds a surprise—an entrancing redhead, claiming Uncle Johnny left his boat to her! Cooper is sure Allie Bateman is a gold digger—and he will do whatever is necessary to win what is rightfully his.

www.eHarlequin.com

HARCNM0508